DEAR BABY

EDITING BY WILLIAM SAROYAN

JULY 4, 1944   LONDON

Dear Baby

By

William Saroyan

hb

Harcourt, Brace and Company, New York

A WARTIME BOOK

PRINTED IN THE UNITED STATES OF AMERICA

This book is for
CAROL SAROYAN

What's said in this small book is not what I would finally say to you, but let it be the first of many gifts of love: a valentine made out of everything I was in the years long gone, before I saw you.

Acknowledgment: Only two or three of the stories in this collection have not appeared at one time or another in one or another of the following living and dead, little and big magazines: *Collier's*, *Harper's Bazaar*, *The Little Man*, *Hairenik* (Armenian-American Weekly of Boston), *The Coast*, *The Yale Review*, Heywood Broun's *Nutmeg*, *transition*, *Rob Wagner's Script*, *Vogue*, and *The Atlantic Monthly*, whose editors I thank.

A number of these pieces have been given new titles and each of them has been revised.

CONTENTS

DEAR BABY

DEAR BABY

The room was a large one on the seventh floor of the Blackstone Hotel on O'Farrell Street in San Francisco. There was nothing in it to bring him there except the portable radio-phonograph, the one record, and darkness.

He came into the room smiling, and walked about, trying to decide what to do. He had six hours to go, and after that a time so long he didn't like to think about it.

He no longer saw the room. During the day the blind of the only window was drawn to keep the place dark. At night he turned the light of the bathroom on and kept the door almost shut so that only enough light came into the room to keep him from walking into something. It happened anyway. It wasn't that he couldn't see as well as ever. It was simply that he was alone again all the time and wasn't looking. There was no longer any reason to look.

He remembered everything.

At the core of everything was his remembrance of her.

He walked about quietly, turning, bumping into the edges of doorways and chairs and other objects in the room, moving unconsciously, his eyes unable to see because of the remembrance. He stopped suddenly, removed his hat and coat, stretched and shook his head as he did when he was confused in the ring.

It was nothing.

He could go on as if he had never known her. He could

be boisterous in act and loud in laughter, and some day be all right again. He could go on like everybody else in the world, but he didn't know if he wanted to. Lazzeri said he was in better shape than ever, but Lazzeri didn't know what he knew.

The odor of her hair, the taste of her mouth, and the image of her face came to him. His guts sickened. He smiled and sat on the bed. After a moment he got up, went to the portable machine, turned the knob, and put needle to disc. Then he stretched out on the bed, face down, and listened to the music, remembering her, and saying: "Dear baby, remembering you is the only truth I know. Having known you is the only beauty of my life. In my heart, there is one smile, the smile of your heart in mine when we were together."

When the telephone rang he knew it was Lazzeri. He got up and turned off the machine.

"Joe?" Lazzeri said.

"Yeah."

"Are you all right?"

"Sure."

"Remember what I told you?"

"What did you tell me?"

"I want you to take it easy."

"That's what I'm doing."

"Don't go haywire."

"O.K."

"What's the matter?"

"I've been sleeping."

"Oh," Lazzeri said. "O.K. I'll see you at nine."

"O.K."

"Something's the matter," Lazzeri said.

"Don't be silly."

"Something's the matter," Lazzeri said again. "I'm coming right up."

"I've been sleeping," Joe said. "I'll see you at nine."

"You don't sound right," Lazzeri said.

"I'm fine."

"You haven't got somebody in that room with you, have you?"

"No."

"Joe," Lazzeri said, "what's the matter?"

"I'll see you at nine," Joe said.

"You're not going haywire on me again, are you?"

"No."

"O.K.," Lazzeri said. "If you're all right, that's all I want to know."

"I'm all right," Joe said.

"O.K.," Lazzeri said. "If you want to be alone, O.K. Just don't go haywire."

"I'll see you at nine," Joe said.

He went back to the machine, turned the knob, and then decided not to listen to the music any more. That's what he would do. He wouldn't listen to the music any more. He would break the record. He would give the machine away. He would lift the blind of the window. He would turn on all the lights and open his eyes. He would come to the room only to sleep. He would go down to the poolroom on Turk Street and find a couple of the boys. He would shoot pool and listen to the boys talking about cards and horses and the other varieties of trouble they knew. He would go up to a couple of the places he used to visit and find some girls he used to know and buy them drinks and ask how they'd been and hear them tell of the troubles *they* knew. He would stop being alone.

He began to laugh, at first quietly and then out loud. He laughed at himself—the wretched comedy of his grief. Then he laughed at everybody alive, and began to feel everything was going to be all right again. If you could laugh, you could live. If you could look at it that way, you could endure *anything*. While he was laughing he heard *her* laughing with him, as clearly as if she were in the room. He became sick again and stopped laughing, knowing it was no use.

He remembered her as if she were still alive, walking beside him along one of many streets in one of many cities, her face childlike and solemn, her movement beside him shy and full of innocence, her voice so young and lovely he would stop anywhere to hold her in his arms while she said seriously: "Joe, people are looking."

He remembered her alone with him in one of many rooms, her presence the first goodness and beauty in his life. He remembered the sweetness of her mouth and the soft hum of her heart growing to the sudden sobbing that brought out in him a tenderness so intense it was ferocious, a tenderness he had always hidden because there had never been anyone to give it to.

He walked about in the dark room, remembering how unkind he had been to her the night he had come home and

6

found her listening to the record. He pointed at the machine and said, "Where did that come from?"

He remembered the way she ran to him and put her arms around him and the way he pushed her away. He remembered the way she moved away from him and said, "I only made a down payment on it. I'll tell them to come and take it back if you want me to. I thought you'd like it."

The record was playing, and although he knew it was something he liked very much, and needed, and should have known long ago, he went on being unkind. She was on the verge of crying and didn't know where to go or what to do. She went timidly to the machine and was going to shut it off when he shouted at her to let it play. She hurried, almost ran, into the other room, and he stood in front of the machine with his hat on and listened to the record until it finished. Then he shut off the machine and went back to town and didn't come home till after five in the morning. She was asleep. He couldn't understand what right he had to know her, to speak to her, to live in the same house with her, to touch her. He bent over her and touched her lips with his own and saw her eyes open. "Please forgive me," he said.

She sat up smiling and put her arms around him, and he kissed her lips and her nose and her eyes and her ears and her forehead and her neck and her shoulders and her arms and her hands, and while he was doing so he said, "Please remember one thing, baby. No matter what I say to you, I love you. I'm liable to go haywire any time, but don't forget that I love you. Please remember that."

He took off his clothes, got into his bed and went to sleep.

7

Dear Baby

When she got in beside him he woke up and embraced her, laughing, while she whispered his name the sorrowful, serious way she always did when she knew he was all right again.

That was in Ventura, where they had taken an apartment because he had three fights coming up in that vicinity: one in Los Angeles, one in Hollywood, and one in Pismo Beach. He let her come to the fight in Hollywood the night he fought Kid Fuente, the Indian, because he knew how much she wanted to see him in the ring. He got her a ringside seat and after the fight she told him she had sat next to Robert Taylor and Barbara Stanwyck and they had been very nice to her.

"I hope you didn't ask them for an autograph," he said, and she became embarrassed and said, "Yes, I did, Joe."

"Well," he said, "they should have asked *you* for one."

"Oh, they were swell," she said. "They sure liked you."

"Oh, sure," he said. "Sure. Sure. That dumb Indian almost ruined me. I don't know how I won. I guess he got tired trying. I'll be punch-drunk in another three or four months."

"You were wonderful in the ring," the girl said.

He remembered the fight because she had talked about it so much. It was six rounds. He was almost out in the fourth. She had known it and kept talking around it, but one day she said, "I almost cried."

"What are you talking about?" he said.

"I mean," she said, "at the fight. Everybody was yelling and I didn't know whether they were for you or against you and I almost cried."

"When was that?" he said.

"I don't know," she said. "I was so excited. He was fighting hard and you were in a corner and everybody stood up and was yelling. I thought he was hitting *me*."

He remembered being in the corner, taking a lot of bad ones, not being able to do anything about them, not knowing if he wasn't going to be out and saying to himself, "You'll be punch-drunk in no time at this rate." He kept trying to move away, but there was nowhere to go, and all of a sudden the Indian slowed down, he was tired, and he remembered saying to the Indian, "O.K., Kid, that's all." He knew he was going to be all right now because there weren't more than fifteen seconds to that round. He gave the rest of the round everything he had. The Indian was tired and couldn't do anything, and just before the bell the Indian stopped a bad one and fell backward, looking up at him with an amazed expression because the Indian couldn't understand how anybody could take so much punishment and come up so strong.

The bell saved the Indian, but for the rest of the fight the Indian was no good, and he knocked him down once in each of the last two rounds.

"That was a bad spot," he told her. "By rights I should have been out, but the Indian got tired. You can't start slugging that way in the middle of a round and expect to keep it up till the end of the round."

"You looked fine," she said, "and you didn't look sore. Don't you get sore?"

"Sore?" he said. "Who's there to get sore at? That poor Indian is only out to earn a little money, the same as me.

9

He's got nothing against me and I've got nothing against him. If he can floor me, he's going to do it, and if I can floor him, I'm going to do it."

"Well," she said, "I almost cried. You looked so fine all the rest of the fight, but when you were in the corner the only thing I could see was somebody being hit over and over again."

"I didn't like that myself," he said.

He was glad she hadn't seen some of his bad fights—the earlier ones, the ones in which he had taken a lot of punishment. Lately he'd learned enough about the racket not to get into a lot of trouble. He seldom took advantage of a chance to clinch, but if the worst came to the worst and there was nothing else to do he would do it, rest a few seconds and try to figure out what to do in the remaining seconds of the round. He usually ended every round nicely, coming back if he had been hurt earlier. Of course he had the reach, his legs were good, and even when he was hurt they didn't wobble and he could stay solid.

After seeing the fight with Kid Fuente she didn't want to see any more. The day of a fight she would be sick, sick in bed, and she would pray. She would turn on the phonograph and listen to the record, which had become their music, the song of their life together. And when he'd come home he'd find her pale and sick and almost in tears, listening to the song. He would hold her in his arms a long time, and he would hear her heart pounding, and little by little it would slow down to almost normal, and then he would hold her at arm's length and look into her eyes and she would be smiling, and then he would say, "It only means fifty dollars extra, baby, but I won." And she'd know there was no vanity in him, she'd understand what he was talking about, and she would ask him what she could get him. Ham and eggs? Scotch and soda? What would he like? She would rush around in an apron and fool around with food and dishes and put the stuff on the table.

He used to eat even if he wasn't hungry. Just so he hadn't lost. If he'd lost, he'd be mean, he'd be so sore at himself that he'd be mean to her, and she wouldn't know what to do, but in the midst of being mean to her he would suddenly say in a loud voice, "And don't be a fool, either; don't pay any attention to anything I'm saying now because I'm out of my head. I made a mess of the whole fight."

When he came home from the fight with Sammy Kaufman of New York he was pretty badly hurt. His head was heavy, his lips were swollen, his left eye was twitching, every muscle of his body was sore, and he was swearing all the time, even though it had been a good fight and a draw.

He wasn't mean to her that night, though, and she said, "Joe, please give it up. You can make money some other way. We don't need a lot of money."

He walked around the apartment and talked to himself. Then suddenly he calmed down and shut off the lights and put the record on the machine and sat down with her to listen to their song. It was a piece by Jan Sibelius, from the *King Kristian Suite,* called "Elegie." He played the record three times, then fell asleep from exhaustion, and she kept playing the record until he woke up a half-hour later. He was smiling, and he said, "I'd like to quit, baby, but I don't know any other way to make money."

Dear Baby

The following week he tried gambling and lost.

After that he had stuck to fighting. They had traveled together up and down the coast—north to San Francisco, Sacramento, Reno, Portland, and Seattle, and then south to the towns along the coast and in the valley that were good fight towns, and Hollywood and Los Angeles and San Diego—when he found out about it. From the beginning he was scared to death, in spite of how good it made him feel. He tried his best not to be scared and tried to keep her in good spirits, but he was worried about it all the time. She was a child herself. She was too little. He didn't know what to do. He remembered her saying one night, "Please let me have it, Joe. I want it so badly."

"Do you think I don't want it?" he said. "Do you think I don't want you to have it? That's *all* I want. That's all I've ever wanted."

Then he began to mumble, talking to himself.

"What, Joe?" she said.

"Do you feel all right?" he said. "Do you feel you can do it? You're not scared, are you?"

"I'm a little scared," she said, "but I guess everybody's scared the first time."

The months of waiting were the happiest of his life. Everything that was good in him had come out—even though he was worried all the time. Even in the ring he had been better than ever. His fights were all good, except one, and that was the fight with the champion, Corbett, which had been a draw, but very close, some sports writers saying he had won and others saying that Corbett had won, and everybody wanting a rematch, especially Lazzeri.

Dear Baby

So tonight he was fighting Corbett again. He had six hours to go. If he won this fight he and Lazzeri would be in the big money at last. He believed he could take the fight, but what if he did? What did he care about money now? Suppose he did take the fight? Where could he go *after* the fight?

"I'm dead," he said. "What's the use bluffing?"

Remembering the girl, he fell asleep, and when he woke up he went to the telephone, without thinking, and asked the hotel operator to get him Corbett at Ryan's Gymnasium, and call him back. A moment later the telephone rang. He answered it, and Corbett said, "Hello, is that you, Joe?"

"Ralph," Joe said, "I want to tell you I'm out to win tonight. I think it's about time you retired."

At the other end of the line Corbett busted out laughing and swore at his friend in Italian.

"I'll take care of you, kid," he said. "You know I like an aggressive fighter."

"Don't say I didn't tell you," Joe said.

"See you in the ring," Corbett said.

In the ring, when they shook hands, Joe said, "This is going to be your last fight." Corbett didn't know he was talking to himself.

"O.K., Joe," he said.

The first round was fast and wild. Even the sports writers couldn't understand. Lazzeri was sore as hell.

"Joe," he said, "what do you think you're doing? You can't beat Corbett that way. Take it easy. Fight *his* fight."

The second round was faster and wilder than the first. They were probably even, but that was only because he

13

wasn't tired yet. The music was humming in him all the time, getting into the roar of the crowd and sweeping along in him, while his heart kept talking to the girl, dreaming that she was still alive, at home listening to their song, waiting for him to come home and take her in his arms.

Lazzeri wanted to hit him after the second round. "Joe," he said, "listen to me. Fight Corbett's fight. He'll kill you."

("That's O.K. with me," his heart said. "Dear Baby, that's O.K. with me.")

The third round, if anything, was faster than the first and second, and coming out of a clinch Corbett said, "What do you think you're doing, Joe?"

"I'm knocking you out," Joe said.

Corbett laughed at him and they began slugging again, one for one, with the sports writers looking at each other, trying to figure out what was going on.

Lazzeri was furious.

"Joe," he said, "I'm not talking to you. I've worked with you six years. I changed you from a punk to a great fighter. Now you're throwing away the championship—the chance we've been working for all these years. You can go to hell, Joe. I hope he floors you in the next round."

During the fourth round things began to go haywire. Corbett's left eye was cut and bleeding badly, and it seemed he was bewildered and less strong than he had been.

("What the hell," his heart said. "Is Corbett going to go haywire at a time like this?")

After the round Lazzeri said, "Joe, I think you've got him—but I'll talk to you later. Your next fight will be in

Madison Square Garden. We'll go to Florida for a while. But I'll talk to you later."

In the fifth round Corbett was slow, his punches were weak and he seemed confused. Toward the end of the round he fell and stayed on one knee to the count of nine.

"You're fighting the most beautiful fight you've ever fought," Lazzeri said. "The sports writers are crazy about you. You're a real champion, Joe."

The fight was stopped near the end of the sixth round because Corbett's eye was so bad.

Lazzeri was crazy with joy but unable to understand what had happened. It was obvious that Joe had fought a great fight—that his style had been perfect for *this* fight. And yet Lazzeri knew something was wrong somewhere.

"Joe," he said in the cab, "you're a champion now. What's eating you?"

"I'm not fighting for three or four months, am I?" he said.

"Two or three, anyway," Lazzeri said. "Why?"

"We've got more money than we've ever had before, haven't we?"

"We've got enough for both of us for two years at least," Lazzeri said. "But why? What are you driving at?"

"Nothing," he said. ("Dear Baby," his heart said.) "I think I'm entitled to a little celebrating."

"Sure, sure," Lazzeri said. "I don't want you to go stale. What do you want?"

"I want laughs," he said. "I'll go up to my room. Get a couple of girls. Bring some Scotch. I want *laughs*."

"Sure," Lazzeri said. "Sure, Joe. We'll have a little

party. I need laughs myself after the scare you gave me."

When he got to his room he turned on all the lights, took the record off the phonograph, and for a moment thought of breaking it. He couldn't, though. He put the record under the bed, as if to hide it. He walked around the room until the sickness caught up with him again, only now it was worse than ever, and he sat down on the bed and began to cry.

When Lazzeri and the two girls came into the room it was dark except for a little light coming from the bathroom. The phonograph was playing, and the fighter was sitting on the bed with his head in his hands and he was crying.

"Get the hell out of here," he said softly.

Without a word Lazzeri led the two girls out of the room. "He'll be all right," he said.

"Dear Baby," the fighter kept saying over and over again.

THE HUMMINGBIRD THAT LIVED THROUGH WINTER

Sometimes even instinct is overpowered by individuality —in creatures other than men, I mean. In men instinct is supposed to be controlled, but whether or not it ever actually is I leave to others. At any rate, the fundamental instinct of most—or all—creatures is to live. Each form of life has an instinctive technique of defense against other forms of life, as well as against the elements. What happens to hummingbirds is something I have never found out— from actual observation or from reading. They die, that's true. And they're born somehow or other, although I have never seen a hummingbird's egg, or a young hummingbird.

The mature hummingbird itself is so small that the egg must be magnificent, probably one of the most smiling little things in the world. Now, if hummingbirds come into the world through some other means than eggs, I ask the reader to forgive me. The only thing I know about Agass Agasig Agassig Agazig (well, the great American naturalist) is that he once studied turtle eggs, and in order to get the information he was seeking, had to find fresh ones. This caused an exciting adventure in Boston to a young fellow who wrote about it six or seven years before I read it, when I was fourteen. I was fourteen in 1922, which goes to show you how unimportant the years are when you're dealing with eggs of any kind. I envy the people who study birds, and some day I hope to find out everything that's known about hummingbirds.

I've gathered from rumor that the hummingbird travels incredible distances on incredibly little energy—what carries him, then? Spirit? But the best things I know about hummingbirds are the things I've noticed about them myself: that they are on hand when the sun is out in earnest, when the blossoms are with us, and the smell of them everywhere. You can hardly go through the best kind of day without seeing a hummingbird suspended like a little miracle in a shaft of light or over a big flower or a cluster of little ones. Or turning like gay insanity and shooting straight as an arrow toward practically nothing, for no reason, or for the reason that it's alive. Now, how can creatures such as that —so delicately magnificent and mad—possibly find time for the routine business of begetting young? Or for the exercise of instinct in self-defense? Well, however it may be, let a good day come by the grace of God, and with it will come the hummingbirds.

As I started to say, however, it appears that sometimes even instinct fails to operate in a specie. Or species. Or whatever it is. Anyhow, when all of a kind of living thing turn and go somewhere, in order to stay alive, in order to escape cold or whatever it might be, sometimes, it appears, one of them does not go. Why he does not go I cannot say. He may be eccentric, or there may be exalted reasons—specific instead of abstract passion for another of its kind—perhaps dead—or for a place. Or it may be stupidity, or stubbornness. Who can ever know?

The Hummingbird

There was a hummingbird once which in the wintertime did not leave our neighborhood in Fresno, California.

I'll tell you about it.

Across the street lived old Dikran, who was almost blind. He was past eighty and his wife was only a few years younger. They had a little house that was as neat inside as it was ordinary outside—except for old Dikran's garden, which was the best thing of its kind in the world. Plants, bushes, trees—all strong, in sweet black moist earth whose guardian was old Dikran. All things from the sky loved this spot in our poor neighborhood, and old Dikran loved *them.*

One freezing Sunday, in the dead of winter, as I came home from Sunday School I saw old Dikran standing in the middle of the street trying to distinguish what was in his hand. Instead of going into our house to the fire, as I had wanted to do, I stood on the steps of the front porch and watched the old man. He would turn around and look upward at his trees and then back to the palm of his hand. He stood in the street at least two minutes and then at last he came to me. He held his hand out, and in Armenian he said, "What is this in my hand?"

I looked.

"It is a hummingbird," I said half in English and half in Armenian. Hummingbird I said in English because I didn't know its name in Armenian.

"What is that?" old Dikran asked.

"The little bird," I said. "You know. The one that comes in the summer and stands in the air and then shoots away.

The one with the wings that beat so fast you can't see them. It's in your hand. It's dying."

"Come with me," the old man said. "I can't see, and the old lady's at church. I can feel its heart beating. Is it in a bad way? Look again, once."

I looked again. It was a sad thing to behold. This wonderful little creature of summertime in the big rough hand of the old peasant. Here it was in the cold of winter, absolutely helpless and pathetic, not suspended in a shaft of summer light, not the most alive thing in the world, but the most helpless and heartbreaking.

"It's dying," I said.

The old man lifted his hand to his mouth and blew warm breath on the little thing in his hand which he could not even see. "Stay now," he said in Armenian. "It is not long till summer. Stay, swift and lovely."

We went into the kitchen of his little house, and while he blew warm breath on the bird he told me what to do.

"Put a tablespoonful of honey over the gas fire and pour it into my hand, but be sure it is not too hot."

This was done.

After a moment the hummingbird began to show signs of fresh life. The warmth of the room, the vapor of the warm honey—and, well, the will and love of the old man. Soon the old man could feel the change in his hand, and after a moment or two the hummingbird began to take little dabs of the honey.

"It will live," the old man announced. "Stay and watch."

The transformation was incredible. The old man kept his hand generously open, and I expected the helpless bird to shoot upward out of his hand, suspend itself in space, and scare the life out of me—which is exactly what happened. The new life of the little bird was magnificent. It spun about in the little kitchen, going to the window, coming back to the heat, suspending, circling as if it were summertime and it had never felt better in its whole life.

The old man sat on the plain chair, blind but attentive. He listened carefully and tried to see, but of course he couldn't. He kept asking about the bird, how it seemed to be, whether it showed signs of weakening again, what its spirit was, and whether or not it appeared to be restless; and I kept describing the bird to him.

When the bird was restless and wanted to go, the old man said, "Open the window and let it go."

"Will it live?" I asked.

"It is alive now and wants to go," he said. "Open the window."

I opened the window, the hummingbird stirred about here and there, feeling the cold from the outside, suspended itself in the area of the open window, stirring this way and that, and then it was gone.

"Close the window," the old man said.

We talked a minute or two and then I went home.

The old man claimed the hummingbird lived through that winter, but I never knew for sure. I saw hummingbirds again when summer came, but I couldn't tell one from the other.

One day in the summer I asked the old man.

"Did it live?"

"The little bird?" he said.

"Yes," I said. "That we gave the honey to. You remember. The little bird that was dying in the winter. Did it live?"

"Look about you," the old man said. "Do you see the bird?"

"I see humming*birds*," I said.

"Each of them is our bird," the old man said. "Each of them, each of them," he said swiftly and gently.

THE STOLEN BICYCLE

This movie of 1919 was full of high spirits, recklessness, and excellent timing, so that when Ike George left the theater he himself was like a man in a movie: full of energy, afraid of nothing, and eager to get on with his life.

As if it were not himself, as if it were not wrong to do so, he took the brand-new bike out of the bicycle rack in front of the theater, and, in full view of the whole world, rode away on it.

Johnny Faragoh, who sold bicycles for Kebo the Jap, was standing in front of his house on L Street.

As the boy rode by, Johnny noticed the new bike.

"Hey, kid!" he called out.

The boy turned in the street and coasted up. He knew Johnny. If he called you, you had to stop. It was a pleasure for the boy, though: he had always admired Johnny, who was like somebody in a movie himself.

"That's a swell bike," Johnny said. "Where'd you get it?"

"Mr. York gave it to me for my birthday," the boy said.

"You mean the guy who's in charge of street sales for *The Herald?*"

"Yeah."

The boy got off the bike and let the older one take the handlebars. Johnny lifted the bike, bounced it, sat on it, and very easily began riding around in a small circle.

23

"He gave you a good one, boy. What's your name?"

"Ike."

"Ike what?"

"Ike George," the boy said.

"You anything to *Cookie* George?"

"He's my cousin."

"First or second?"

"First."

"Cookie's a good friend of mine," Johnny said.

"He's always in trouble," Ike said.

"Where'd you steal it?" Johnny said. "You can tell *me*."

"I didn't steal it," Ike said. "Mr. York gave it to me for my birthday."

"Cookie's my pal," Johnny said. "Somebody else gave it to you. That guy York wouldn't give you a bike if you saved his life."

"He gave me *this* bike," the boy said.

"Tell them Cookie gave it to you," Johnny said. "Somebody'll go and ask York and you'll get in trouble."

"Cookie's got no money," the boy said.

"Sometimes he has and sometimes he hasn't," Johnny said. "I'm going to see him tonight," Johnny said. "I'll tell him about it. Go on home now."

The boy got on the bicycle and rode home.

When his father saw the bicycle he said, "Haig, where did you get that bicycle?"

"Cookie gave it to me," the boy said.

"You mean your cousin Gourken?"

"Yes," the boy said.

"Gourken has no money," the boy's father said. "You've borrowed it, haven't you?"

"No," the boy said. "It's mine."

"Go inside and eat your supper," the father said.

The boy went inside and ate his supper. It took him less than five minutes. When he came out of the house his father was riding the bike in the yard.

"Haig," the father said, "take the bicycle back where you got it. You're no thief."

"Cookie gave it to me," the boy said.

The next day he rode the bicycle to school, just the way it was. He didn't turn it over and hammer out the numbers the way you were supposed to do. The numbers were 137620R. After school he rode the bicycle to *The Evening Herald,* and told everybody his cousin Cookie had given it to him for a birthday present.

"What's your birthday?" his friend Nick Roma asked him.

"September 7, 1909," the boy said.

"This is May," Nick said. "You'll get in trouble, Ike."

He rode the bicycle to his corner, Mariposa and Eye, and sold papers all afternoon. Cookie came to the corner in the evening. "Is this the bike?" he said.

"Yeah," the boy said.

"I sure gave you a good one, didn't I?"

"Yeah. Thanks."

By October he had almost forgotten how the bicycle had come into his possession. In November the chain broke while he was sprinting. The rim of the front wheel broke and the fork buckled. It cost him a dollar-and-a-quarter for a new rim. Another dollar to have the buckled fork replaced by a straight secondhand one, and fifty cents for labor.

After that the bike was his, out and out.

One day a year after he had taken the bike from the rack in front of the Liberty Theatre, he put it back into the rack, and went on in and saw the show.

When he came out, the bike was gone. He walked home, and when he saw his father he said, "They stole my bike."

"That's all right," his father said. "Go inside and eat your supper."

"I'm not hungry," the boy said. "If I catch the fellow who stole it, I'll give him the worst beating he ever got."

"Go inside and eat," the boy's father said.

"I don't want to eat," the boy said.

He stood before his father, very angry, and then suddenly turned and ran. He ran all the way to town and walked along every street looking for his bike. After an hour he walked home, ate his supper, and went to bed.

He was now eleven years old.

One evening in August he was playing handball with Nick Roma against the wall of the Telephone Building. Nick made a man-killer, a truck turned into the alley, bumped the ball, and carried it down the alley. The boy went after the ball. It had fallen down a small flight of stairs into a narrow passageway where there were garbage cans and boxes full of ashes. He looked for the ball. In a corner he saw a bicycle frame, with the paint scratched off. He turned the frame upside down and read the number. It had been hammered, but he could still read the 13 and the R.

He stood in the dark passageway, holding the old frame. His friend Nick Roma came up and said, "Where's the ball?"

"It's lost," the boy said. "I found my bike. They took everything off of it."

"Is the frame all right?" Nick said.

"It's all right," the boy said, "but what good is a frame without the other stuff?"

"It's worth *something*," Nick said.

"I'd like to get the guy who stole it," the boy said.

Paul Armer came walking down the alley and saw the two boys with the bicycle frame.

He examined the frame with them.

"What do you want for it, Ike?" he said.

"I don't know," the boy said.

He was angry and broken-hearted.

"It was my bike," he said to Paul. "Then they stole it. We were playing handball, I went to get the ball and I found the frame. They took everything off of it and threw it in here."

"Where did the ball go?" Nick said.

"To hell with the ball," Ike said.

"I'll give you a dollar for it," Paul Armer said.

"All right," the boy said.

A week later when he saw the bike again, painted and with new parts, he became angry again and said to himself, "If I ever get the guy who stole it!"

KNIFE-LIKE, FLOWER-LIKE, LIKE NOTHING AT ALL IN THE WORLD

"He'll be around any minute now," Max said. "I give you my word. He'll be here."

The little man at the table nodded as Max spoke, and Max said to himself, as he wiped the bar, "What's he want to see a guy like Pete for?"

A good-looking woman came in and ordered a Scotch and soda, and while he was getting the drink Max went on talking to the little man.

"It's none of my business," he said, "but what do you want to see Pete for?"

"I beg your pardon?" the lady said.

"Oh," Max said. "Excuse me, lady. I was talking to the little fellow at the table over there." ("Little fellow at the table?" Max repeated to himself. "What the hell kind of talk is that?")

"He's a friend of mine," the lady said.

"No, no," Max said quickly. "I was talking to that little gentleman over there." ("Little gentleman? Why couldn't he leave out the *little* part of it?")

"Well," the lady said, "even so. He's a friend of mine."

"Who?" Max said.

28

"Pete," the lady said.

The little man got up from the table and went to the bar. He studied the woman, and tried to smile.

(What's this? Max thought.)

"I'm his father," the little man said.

The woman turned and looked down at the little man. It seemed to Max that she didn't think very much of him.

"His *father?*" the woman said.

"Yes," the little man said. "Pete Morgan."

"My name is Ethel Beede," the woman said. The way she said the last name Max knew it had an extra "e" in it somewhere and that, most likely, as he put it, she stank. She didn't exactly stink, but he knew what he meant.

"My name is Henry," the little man said.

"How do you do," the woman said.

"Thank you," the little man said. "I came here tonight to see Pete. He hasn't been home in two weeks."

Max couldn't figure it out.

Pete showed up every night sometime between midnight and two, but he was always alone. Tonight his father shows up a little after ten, and a little after eleven a woman almost old enough to be his mother shows up, too.

"Your son," the woman said, "is a very interesting young man."

"I've known him all his life," the little man said quietly. "I can imagine he's *fascinating* to people who haven't."

"I'm quite interested in his ambition," the woman said.

"That's very kind of you," the little man said. "What ambition is that?"

"I understand he wants to be an actor," the woman said.

"He has a number of ambitions," the little man said. "Precocious boys generally do."

"He said he was twenty-one," the woman said.

"He's not quite seventeen," the little man said.

"Wait a minute," Max said. "Not quite seventeen? He's been coming in here every night for two weeks. I can't serve drinks to minors. It's against the law. I thought he was twenty-two or twenty-three."

"No," the little man said. "He's not quite seventeen."

The little man hoped the woman would go away and give him a chance to sit down and talk to Pete alone, but the woman didn't seem to want to go.

"He's not quite seventeen," the little man said again.

"I heard you," the woman said.

"Pete is the kind of boy who demands a great deal," the little man said. "Have you been giving him money?"

The woman was not upset by this question, as Max expected her to be.

"Yes, I have," she said.

"You're married," the little man said.

"I beg your pardon?" the woman said.

"Well, to put it another way," the little man said, "you have children, haven't you?"

"I have a daughter nineteen years old," the woman said, "and another seven years old. Give me another Scotch and soda."

Max made another drink for the lady. The little man wasn't drinking.

"Your husband is a wealthy man," Pete's father said.

"*I* am wealthy," the woman said. "My husbands have all been—poor."

"You want to adopt Pete?" the little man said.

"I *beg* your pardon!" the woman said this time. She was really burned up now. (Well, what do you know about that? Max thought. A crazy good-looking punk like Pete —well, for the love of Mike.)

"I only want to warn you," the little man said, "that my son will make you unhappy. I want you to know that you won't hurt *him*. I think he's capable of doing anything. I think he could do something very great or something very strange. I think he could commit murder and not feel guilty. I'm sure you don't know him as well as I do. I want him to take his time and after a while find out for himself what he wants to do. He's restless and bored and pretty angry deeply. I think he can do anything."

"I'm afraid I don't understand," the woman said.

"I'm very fond of Pete," the little man said. "Maybe it's because he's not like me or his mother or any of his brothers and sisters. We're all very fond of him, but *me* most of all. Pete's ashamed of me, I'll tell you that. At the same time I think he likes me more than he likes any other person in the world. I'm sure you don't intend to marry Pete."

(Well, for crying out loud, Max thought. The people you run into in a little bar.)

"We're going to be married day after tomorrow," the woman said.

"I see," the little man said.

"We're very much in love," the woman said. She was deeply hurt. Even Max could tell that. Well, as far as Max was concerned, if she *had* to marry somebody she could pick on somebody her size, somebody like himself.

(Oh, oh, Max thought suddenly. One of these two ought to get out of here in a hurry. That kid will be coming in here any minute now.)

"He'll be coming in here any minute now," he said. He wiped the bar as he spoke, so the remark wouldn't be too bald, or whatever it was.

"Yes, I know," the little man said. He turned to the woman. "I've always encouraged Pete to do whatever he's felt like doing," he said. "I'll pretend I didn't know, and after it's over I'll convince his mother not to interfere, too."

"You're very kind," the woman said.

She was irritated and, it seemed to Max, a little ashamed.

"I'm thinking of Pete," the little man said.

He turned and walked out of the place without another word. Max got busy with some glasses at the other end of the bar.

"Give me another Scotch and soda," the woman said.

She was sore and ashamed and she looked ugly all of a sudden. At first she had seemed rather beautiful, or at least striking, but now all of a sudden when Max looked at her she looked awful. Max put her drink down in front of her and went over to the phonograph and put in a nickel.

When the record ended Max put in another nickel. The kid ought to be in any minute now. He kept looking toward the door and feeling uncomfortable. The woman kept trying not to look toward the door. Max kept putting nickels in the phonograph and looking toward the door.

At two o'clock he said, "It's closing time, lady."

32

The woman paid for nine Scotch and sodas and began to go. Near the door she turned around and came back.

("That's right, lady," Max said to himself. "I'm not seventeen, but I'm not so bad. I'm only forty-eight. Let's talk this thing over. If you've got to marry somebody, marry somebody your size. Marry me.")

Max leaned over the bar toward the lady, who crumpled a bill in her hand and, shaking Max's hand, left the bill in it and turned to go. At the door she stopped again. (And Max said to himself, "Come on, lady. Think this thing over. You're tight and I'm big and—discreet, too.") The woman came over to Max again.

"We're very much in love with one another," she said. ("I'll say we are," Max said. "Lady, you've got no idea how much in love with one another we are. Just say the good word.")

"Lady," Max said. He felt silly.

The woman moved closer to him, waiting.

"Yes?" she said.

"I'm sorry," Max said. "This is the first night in two weeks that he's not been in."

"It's all right," the woman said.

"Can I help you to a cab?"

"My car's outside."

"I'd be glad to drive you home," Max said. "I mean—"

"My chauffeur's in the car," the woman said.

The woman went out before Max had a chance to get around the bar and open the door for her. He went to the door and locked it and while he did so he saw the chauffeur open the door of the car, help the woman in, and then drive away.

Max stood at the door about three minutes. (What's the matter with *me?* he thought.) He returned to the bar and put away everything for the night. He put on his coat, and then poured himself a little drink, which he sipped thoughtfully.

The door rattled but he didn't even think of hollering out that he was closed for the night.

The door rattled again and then he heard Pete shout, "Hey, Max! Let me in a minute."

Max went to the door and opened it and Pete came in.

"Max," he said. "Give me a drink. Something's happened. I'm in love."

"Yeah, I know," Max said.

"*You* know?" Pete said. "I just met her tonight."

"*Met who?*" Max said.

"Max, I met the most beautiful girl in the world," Pete said. "She's just a kid, but she's wonderful. She's innocent and simple and—well, by God, I'm not ashamed to say it—wonderful."

"You said wonderful before," Max said.

"She's fourteen years old," Pete said. "Where do you think I found her?"

Max began to think.

"In a movie?" he said.

"No," Pete said. "I went home tonight instead of keeping an appointment. So I decided to stop at the florist's on the corner and take the folks some flowers. I found her in the florist's. She's his daughter. Half Irish, half Italian.

34

Beautiful. Quiet. Lonely. I bought the flowers and took them home and sat around talking, waiting for my father to come home. He'd gone back to the office to do some overtime. So, after a while I went back to the florist's and met her father and her mother and asked them if I could take her to the neighborhood movie. After the movie I took her home and I've been walking around town ever since."

"I see," Max said. "That's swell."

"How've things been?" Pete said.

"Not bad."

"Anybody been around?"

"A few people I don't know."

"Any interesting barroom talk?"

"Some."

"I'm going to open a bar myself some day," Pete said. "I like to see all kinds of people and hear them talk."

"Is that so?" Max said.

"Yeah," Pete said. "The variety, Max. All the different people alive. All the different faces. All the different ways of talking. I like to listen to the way they *laugh*, especially. Do you know how *she* laughs?"

"No," Max said.

"Like an angel," Pete said. "It breaks my heart. It makes me sadder than anything in the world. I'm in love with her, but the only trouble is the world's full of them."

"That's right," Max said.

"That's the only trouble," Pete said. "There are so many of them."

"There sure are plenty of them," Max said.

"They're all over the place," Pete said. "Anywhere you

go. This one was in the florist's, right in my block. Think of all the other blocks. All the other cities. The hundreds of thousands of them."

"Yeah," Max said. He felt old and grateful for a little place of his own and easy working hours and easy work and a place to sleep and an old indifference about the hundreds of thousands of them.

"Yeah," he said. "That's right, Pete."

Pete swallowed another drink and tossed a dollar on the bar.

"On me tonight," Max said.

"Thanks," Pete said. "See you tomorrow—" he began to say. He stopped. "I may not be around again for a while," he said. "It's about three miles from here to my neighborhood."

"O.K.," Max said.

"So long," Pete said.

Max watched him walk away swiftly, like somebody in a play. He put on his hat and let himself out and locked the door. He began to walk slowly around the corner, more grateful than ever for the old indifference, and yet for some reason a little irritated with his comfortable life.

THE DREAM

She was twelve then and just beginning to suspect, but she didn't know. There was the dream, and then suddenly in the midst of it there was poetry, or rather one poem. By P. B. Shelley. In which the fountains, as you may remember, mingle with the river, the rivers with the ocean, the winds of heaven with a sweet emotion. Suddenly, in the midst of the sweetness of summer, the smell of living in the cool of evening, there was poetry, and the gentle joyous grieving of her heart as she remembered things dreamed or guessed.

She was a plain girl, even then, but not the plainest in the world. The worst thing, which was not part of the plainness, which, in fact, just kept her from being a plain beauty, a girl of much natural charm and very good spirits, was her eyes. The huge, bulging, leaping, wonderful eyes, so wide-open and perfect, so completely complete, so final in themselves, so very separate from all the rest of her, so forward and startled, so unnecessary to such a small and otherwise dainty face, and so frightening to herself.

In many of her dreams, in many of the love ones even, in many of the ones in which she walked out fearlessly to her love and took his hand, was the terrible remembrance of her eyes and her fear that he would be frightened by them. But for years he wasn't. For years he knew only of the wonderful things: her wonderful stillness, her wonderful innocence, her wonderful smell, her wonderful hands, the wonderful taste of her mouth, and all the other wonderful things.

And then one year it happened.

It was the year she was seventeen. That year he looked into her eyes. She screamed in terror and ran away. He knew. He had seen. And *she* had seen his face when he had seen. She had clapped her hands over her eyes and then she had screamed and fled.

By the time she was twenty she'd decided she was hopeless when it came to that.

There were other things, thank God. She proceeded to find them, and one by one, one after another, she did. She found each of the other things, and for a time each was wonderful. She went to all the lectures on poetry, painting, music, and sculpture; to all the concerts, the operas, the ballets, the theaters, and so on and so forth.

Later, she decided to make it more personal and try to do something herself, dip the brush in paint, and put the wet brush to canvas. After painting came writing.

All this time the dream was lonely for her, but she was too busy to pay any attention to it. Sometimes in the summer she got up a little before daybreak and went out and walked, almost dancing with energy. In the wintertime the dream grew more real in the deeper sleep of the white sleep-stricken season.

The years of writing were by far the closest to anything like reality. Like real fun, real delight, real eagerness and enjoyment. Of course her writing wasn't published—because, she felt, it was new. But also because it would be humiliating to offer her work to editors and have it turned down. This attitude ended after two years of writing when she decided if one was a writer one needed to be published and read. She had gone to a number of gatherings of writers and others in the Village and had heard this theory discussed many times. Most of the writers were sure it didn't matter at all if what you wrote got published or not, just so it was great, but one night a young Bulgarian named Marek Valentin got drunk and *proved* to them all that they were wrong, and a pack of posers.

She was shocked at the time, but many weeks later she forgot his vulgarity and knew he was right. The next thing she wrote she sent to a magazine, and for many weeks worried about what would happen to it. It came back, with a printed slip of paper clipped to it. She sat down and cried and remembered and cried and looked at the writing which was suddenly so ugly, and then she grew angry and *really* began to cry because she knew she wasn't a writer.

But she tried again. It wasn't money she wanted at all. She would give *them* money. She would give them any amount of it they wanted if it would be for a good cause, if it would be to start a new and really good magazine, something that would lift literature out of the decay it had fallen into. If it would carry literature out of the machinery it had gotten caught in.

She went to the gatherings almost every time they asked her. Everyone liked to tell her his troubles and how bitter it was to be great and yet unknown and poor. She was only too glad to help. It was a privilege and it made her very happy because it was all so secret and informal and exciting. Everyone was fond of her.

They talked things over and decided to call the new magazine *The New Magazine* because everyone felt that that was both direct and descriptive. Seven issues were printed in two years. Thousands of manuscripts came in from all over the country and were rejected by the editors. Four issues of the magazine contained work of her own. Most of the other things were by the others. The magazine was attacked on all sides, but only once. It sold very poorly in the four New York bookstores and in the other stores in Boston, Chicago, and San Francisco. In all, sixty subscriptions came in. Several unsuccessful attempts were made to get publishers to advertise in the magazine.

The total cost, however, was negligible: a thousand dollars an issue.

Several of the writers went on and had things accepted by other magazines, and one writer sold an essay to *The American Mercury* for $150, but it was about how to start a new magazine on somebody else's money and print your own writing, the writing of your wife, your wife's cousin, and other friends and relatives.

The essay appeared toward the end.

She felt that the magazine had failed, because literature was still not lifted out of the decay it had fallen into, and because no great American genius had been discovered by the magazine, as they were all so sure he would be.

For a time they were all excited about a boy of nineteen in Lincoln, Nebraska, and believed he was their man, but he wasn't. He was good for the two stories, but no more.

They all wrote to him. They all urged him to go on, that he must, that he owed it to America, that nothing should stop him. But he didn't even answer their letters. She decided to go to Lincoln and find him. He was very disappointing. A small, tense, undernourished Polish boy with a hateful face and no understanding at all. He smoked cigarettes all the time and swore a good deal and said he didn't know what made him write the two stories. He was interested in other things. Real things, he said, and she understood all too well what he meant. He was an awful nasty young man.

After the magazine she decided to travel again. But this time not blindly, but as a writer, with her eyes open.

Back in Paris she went to the kind of neighborhood a writer belonged in, and wrote a little every day.

She was now forty and, as at twelve, suspected but didn't really know.

The dream, dimmer now and more complex, continued and was occasionally twelve years old.

One evening in September, walking through the Quarter, he arrived at last and, in the strangest way imaginable, she was lovely for him. He was from a little town in Arizona and he made it very easy for her to be lovely for him. He was not a writer, he was a painter. He didn't want to have anything to do with words. They had confounded life. He despised them. He had been in Paris a month and this was the first time he had spoken to anyone at any length. They talked a little in French, and a little in English. Of course he was homesick, but he knew that that was absurd. He was rather gay, too. But most important of all he behaved as if he believed she was possibly a woman and took her hand without embarrassment to himself or to her. He really took it, with her really giving it to him, like everything she had to give.

He wasn't *terribly* attractive outwardly, but he was, *really*. They had supper together and the whole thing made her laugh, because it was so wonderful. It was all fine and vital and like loving and being loved. The very eating of the food, and the drinking of the wine, was.

He was just the way she believed he would be. Casual, wise, human, full of contradictions, comical, and sorrowful. It was then most like loving and being loved—when he was sorrowful.

Alone with her, he was awfully sorrowful and his hands began to hold her everywhere. It was amazing that she could scarcely wait and wanted him to tear things off instead of fooling with the buttons and clasps that were so hard for a man to find, and as his hands trembled, the dream leaped up out of its depth and began to clamor for its reality, and she herself became crazy with delight, her fingers cutting into his flesh. It was a struggle for him because of the way she was, but he was good and enjoyed the struggle until she was truly, most beautifully, loving and being loved, wondering where she had mislaid everything, knowing how silly she had been, delighting in the sweet pain, the fountains mingling with the river, the river with the ocean, the mine with thine, and then the heavenly violence, the sweet giving over of the dream, the poetry, and the years, the last and most glorious moment of them all, with the tongue at last saying no word, but being all language.

He said nothing. He was one who didn't talk, who despised words. And she understood his not talking. *He* didn't need to talk. He kissed her and went away. Her eyes hadn't troubled him at all. He had made her forget them.

The next day the waiting was sweet, but in the evening it began to be painful. The sleeping of the night was waiting too, and all the dream could say was his name. In the morning, fully awake, the name was still all the dream could say. The dream took full possession of her now and could say only his name all the time. But he was a painter, and he had work to do. She must be pleased about this and she must be pleased to wait until he came again.

She was pleased to wait three days more and then she was ill. She began to wonder if it had been the same for him as it had been for her, and if, after all, he wasn't simply a lonely young man who had needed her very much at the time. She even began to wonder if it wasn't a little absurd for her to imagine that he would come back, since he was at least ten years younger. She had to decide after another day that she didn't care about that, it didn't matter at all. She spent hours trying to become lovely, and then she went out and began to walk. She went out only to walk, but suddenly she was at the door and full of fear, begging everything in the world to make him be there and make him want her, but the woman who came to the door was sure she was mistaken, there was no one by that name living in her house, there were no Americans at all living in her house, there had *never* been any Americans living in her house, and she kept asking if the house was the number he had given and the lady kept saying it was, and then she kept asking if the street was the street he had given and the lady kept saying it was, and then she began to know that now, at a time like this, she was dying and would most certainly die if the dream could not stop merely *saying* his name.

It could not, though. The dream waited with her, saying the name always, but he did return to her. The illness was terrible and as great a thing in its way as loving and being loved had been. It was full of an ugly wretchedness of loving and being loved, and yet not loving and not being loved. She felt the ugly loving of the infinitely greater body, possessing her infinitely more completely, taking her always and giving nothing. Of course she was ill, too. Physically ill. She had had no food, no sleep, and no rest. The ugly loving kept taking her, until at last she decided it would be better to *let* it take her, to *give* it everything, the dream, the poetry, and all the years. And then, early one morning, she closed her eyes in the dream and was shaken by the wonderful violence she had always suspected and only ten days ago had begun to know, and this time it was infinitely more terrible and beautiful than the first time.

In the dream when she opened her eyes she was instantly blinded, the dream was driven out of her, and all that was left was the poor body in the bed, still alive, but apparently dying swiftly.

A TIME OF GENIUS

They wanted to be alone. He knew that, but it just didn't seem rude to intrude because it seemed there would be certain subtle compensations for them, and then of course after dinner they could go right on. They said they didn't mind at all.

They weren't out and out strangers. They were only people he didn't know very well. They were on the third item, so he told the waiter to bring him the same, the first three together, so he could catch up with them. This was done, and they finished dinner together. He did all the talking, and they thought he was stupid. He could see they thought that, but that didn't matter either. They were a writer and his girl. The girl was studying art. He was as polite as the circumstances called for, asking first about the writer's writing and then about the girl's art. After that the subject was himself exclusively.

Everything was all set. He knew the next hour would bring a lot of small drama around him, and he wanted witnesses.

First the waiter revealed himself to be an unsuccessful student of the horses, a lover of great music, and a man who hated miserliness. His name was August, and he took pride in not having dropped a fork in twenty-seven years of waiting table. In the midst of this modest taking of pride he dropped a knife. He picked it off the floor.

"Knife," he said. "Not fork."

In the kitchen somebody tipped over a stove and dropped a great deal of silverware. Everybody in the restaurant leaped to his feet. August came out of the kitchen and said it was nothing, although the floor was on fire and the chef had fainted.

The young woman found an insect in the broccoli.

A small dog came in from the street with a lady and a gentleman and refused to leave his side, although he didn't throw it a bone. There were no bones.

Then a woman of considerable unattractiveness appeared from somewhere and asked how he'd been. He told her not bad. She then inquired about Ethie. He told her Ethie was well again, and sent her her love. The woman was delighted to see him looking so well and to hear that Ethie was fine. A small man came and took her by the hand. She went away, throwing kisses. The young man and the young woman wanted to know who she was. He mentioned the name of a woman prominent in society who had been married five times because he didn't know.

They were sitting two tables from the window on the street. A boy of nine or ten, a street-boy, a boy in rags, came to the window and for about three full minutes looked in. (Christ, he thought, he hates all of us. He's hungry and he's come to watch us glut ourselves. He's going to be a writer. He'll write a Christmas story in about nine years. He'll write something better than "The Match Girl.") One of the waiters went to the window and motioned the boy to go away. He would have asked the boy to supper, but he didn't have five thousand dollars to go with the gesture, and he couldn't let the boy be embarrassed by human cuteness. The waiter was very angry, but the boy refused to go away.

The waiter decided to ignore the boy, who continued to study the scene. The fire on the floor of the kitchen was put out and the chef was brought to. He came out and shook hands with some well-to-do people. He noticed the boy at the window. How could he help noticing the boy, unless he was deaf, since the boy had been tapping on the window for half a minute?

The chef was very angry. "Go away," he shouted, but the boy only shouted back at him. At first nobody could hear him, but soon everybody heard what the boy was shouting.

"What time is it?" he shouted. "What the hell time is it?"

The chef shouted back that it was eleven minutes past nine.

The boy went away.

Time? What did the boy want with the time, from a restaurant full of people, eating? Was he going to be a difficult writer to read? What was he going to do with information like that? Who was that great writer? What the hell would he be likely to get for wit like that?

THE STORY OF THE YOUNG
MAN AND THE MOUSE

A week of drinking turned the young man's fancy to mice, *the* mouse, the one and only, the mouse of all mice, the city mouse, the brilliant mouse, the genius of mice, the Great Northern Hotel mouse.

He, or it, arrived one night prancing in the manner of an overjoyed retriever. The mouse came fearlessly to the young man and dropped the money at his feet. The money was four ten-dollar bills which the mouse carried in its mouth. The mouse carried the money so dexterously, or rather so magnificently, so thoughtfully, so delicately that not even slight teeth marks impaired the beauty of the money. The young man picked up the money casually, examined it, and studied the mouse, which stood by in perfect harmony with everything.

The young man moved two paces and also stood by in perfect harmony with everything.

"Well," he said. "This *is* delightful."

He looked at the mouse thoughtfully.

"Stealing, hey?" he said.

The mouse nodded the way a clown nods when he acknowledges the commission of some petty but delightful crime.

"All right," the young man said. "I believe in live and let live. You bring me money this way so I can live and

I'll try not to improve your morals. If you want to steal, that's all right with me."

This arrangement appeared to be all right with the mouse, which continued exploring the rooms of the hotel, going to those places where traveling people or retired army officers or people taking a shower like to leave their folding money. Almost every day the mouse returned to the room of the young man to deposit various foldings of American currency: sometimes tens, sometimes fives, sometimes a five and a couple of ones, and one day four ones, which was a crisis and a bitter disappointment to the young man, who was drinking a great deal.

"Live and let live of course," he said to the mouse, "but you can do better than that. Now, let me explain. This number. That's ten. That's good. Get that kind when you can. This is five. Half as good. If you can't get tens, get fives. This is a two. Bad luck. Don't leave them, but they aren't so good. This is one. Awful. Try for tens."

The mouse accepted this simple instruction and was lucky enough to enter rooms where guests who were having showers had left big folding money lying around here and there, so that for many days the young man lived pretty much like a king. He bought clothes. Odds and ends. Ate well. And drank exceptionally well.

The mouse, however, lived on very feeble fare. Old stockings.

"Now," the young man said one day to the mouse, "this may get around. Folks may begin to get suspicious. There is no law against a mouse stealing money, and you'll always be innocent according to the statutes. There isn't a jury in the country that would convict you. But some busybody somewhere may take a long-shot chance and set a trap. They're horrible things, but very attractive outwardly. Cheese is involved. With only one of these pieces of paper which you have just fetched I could buy, I believe, close to twenty pounds of the finest cheese imaginable—which, I daresay, you wouldn't like. They'll try to attract you with cheap cheese. Ten cents a pound. Something like that. Something I haven't eaten in months. Don't be a fool. Don't get taken in. Don't swoon and move into the trap because the smell of the cheese is so wonderful. I'm counting on you to stay in good health."

The mouse had never heard.

Cheese?

Traps?

He didn't know. It was all very exciting.

Money, for some reason, he *did* know. It didn't smell good. It was tasteless and official, but even so.

The young man might have furnished the mouse a little cheese, but he was afraid that if he did the mouse would cease to appreciate anything but food. That, he didn't want. It would be better for the mouse to fend for itself.

"But," he said clearly, "stay away from little pieces of cheese artfully attached to gadgets which appear to be perfectly static and harmless. Once you swoon, you're a goner. It may mean death."

Death?

The mouse hadn't heard.

The drinking continued. Many times the mouse went away and returned with money, but one day the mouse

50

didn't return. Soon the young man began to be poor again. He began to be a little worried, too. First he worried about how he was ever going to be able to keep up appearances without money, but little by little he began to worry about the mouse. In a psychic or alcoholic way, he was able to trace the mouse's course from his room two days ago to where it had fallen into a trap.

This was room 517, one floor down, two doors to the left. The room was inhabited by an old woman whose children sometimes took her to Larchmont for week-ends.

It was a little difficult getting in through the window, but he made it, and sure enough in the corner of the room was the mouse. The old woman was in Larchmont.

The young man burst into tears.

"I told you," he wept. "You see what happens? Now look at you. Here. Let me get you out of this God-damned gadget."

He got the mouse out of the trap and carried it carefully in the palm of his left hand to his room, taking the elevator and weeping.

The elevator boy burst into tears with the young man, but suggested heat and quiet.

Heat and quiet were provided the mouse, and five cents' worth of cheese, which the mouse did not wish to eat.

This frightened the young man.

"Those ungodly people," he said again and again.

The mouse watched the young man quietly for five days and five nights, and then it died.

The young man wrapped it carefully in hotel stationery,

appropriately white, and carried it to Central Park where he dug a small grave with the toe of his right shoe, and buried it.

He returned to the hotel and checked out, complaining bitterly about the type of people inhabiting the world.

THE STRUGGLE OF JIM
PATROS WITH DEATH

Jim Patros is a waiter at Omar Khayyam's in San Francisco. He is a good-natured Greek of forty-four who seems a good deal younger. He is a little under medium-size, but not quite small enough to be a small man. He is well-built, and waits table with efficiency and style. He knows how to be helpful without being obtrusive, and his manners are naturally good.

Like many people who work for a humble living, he is a gambler and feels that some day he is going to make a killing and have all the money he wants. He follows the horses every day, and sits down to a game of stud now and then. So far his luck hasn't been the best in the world, but every six or seven days one of his long-shots comes in and keeps his faith.

And like most people who have always been too busy to loaf, Jim is full of stories about himself.

I like best his story of the time he nearly died of influenza, in Chester, Pennsylvania, in 1918.

I was sick, he said. When I got up in the morning I felt weak, but I put on my clothes, to go to work. When I was putting on my pants I fell down, but I got up. When I was walking to the door I fell down again. I didn't know what it was. I couldn't stand up. The rule was if you was working for the government and you didn't show up for work, they sent somebody to ask what's the matter? I tried to get up but I was too weak. I crawled to the bed and fell on it. The next day the nurse came and said, "What's the matter?"

"I don't know," I said. "I'll come to work tomorrow."

She gave me an examination and said I must go to the hospital. I got up from the bed and said, "I will go to work now." But I fell down, so the nurse helped me and said, "Well, stay in bed, anyway."

In the afternoon, the landlady came and said, "My boy, how are you?"

"Mother," I said, "I do not know."

There was a Greek doctor from Smyrna, so I said, "Mother, tell the doctor to come and look at me."

When the doctor from Smyrna came, the government doctor with the nurse was telling the landlady I must go to the hospital, but I said, "Let my countryman see me."

So the Greek doctor looked at me. He told me to go to the hospital. So. If I am sick, I got to go to the hospital, but I said, "No. I will stay here."

They went away, but an hour later came the police patrol and the government doctor and two policemen, and the nurse, and she said, "Get up."

"What for?" I said. "I work for the government."

"We know," they said. "We got orders. We must take you to the hospital."

"No," I said. "I want to go back to work."

So I got up again, but I couldn't walk. So. If I am sick, I got to go to the hospital.

The Struggle of Jim Patros with Death

"Take me in a boat to the best hospital in Philadelphia," I said.

"All the hospitals in Philadelphia are full," the doctor said. "We'll take care of you."

So they took me in the police patrol to the hospital. But what is the hospital?

Stable. One big room, with an *aisley* down the middle and beds on both sides. They put me in a bed and I began to wait. Three days they gave me nothing to eat and no water to drink. Only smashed ice. One night I see the nurse bringing food, but what is it? Fishes' tails. The nurse put down the dish and I looked at the fishes' tails.

"What is this?" I said.

"Food," the nurse said.

"Food?" I said. "Please. Take it away."

I began to look around and think about it. "What kind of a place is this?" I said. "What's the fishes' tails for?"

There was a dark nurse there who looked like a Greek, so I called her.

"Are you Greek?" I said.

"I am Serbian," the nurse said.

"I don't like this place," I said. "Do they want to kill us?"

She told me in this place they pushed them out. They were all too sick. All the hospitals were full, and everybody was dying. But this place was the worst. If I'm going to die, I'm going to die at home, not in a slaughterhouse.

"I am Greek," I said to the nurse. "I want to go home. Tonight you bring my clothes and I get dressed and go home."

"If I lose my job," the nurse said, "I will do it. Do you think you will be able to walk?"

"I'll walk," I told her. "Please bring my clothes."

So. In the night she brought my clothes and helped me put them on. When I tried to stand up I began to fall, so she helped me. Everybody was sick, but they knew what I was doing.

"Jim," they said. "Where you going?"

"I'm going home," I said. "If I'm going to die, I'm going to die at home."

I tried to walk but I fell down, and the Serbian girl began to cry.

"Please try to walk," she said.

She walked with me to the door. In front of my eyes I couldn't see, but she stayed by me until I got a little fresh air. Then I could see, but what could I see?

All snow.

"How will you get home?" the girl said.

"I'll get home," I said.

She closed the door and went back. I sat down on the steps and my eyes began to close. I began to dream about the days in Greece when I used to run in the hills and eat berries and drink water from the rivers. Then somebody put his hand on my shoulder. It was an officer in the army.

"What's the matter?" he said.

"I'm going home," I said.

"Do you belong in this hospital?" he said.

"This is not a hospital," I said. "This is a slaughterhouse."

"Come to my office," he said.

In the office he said, "Sit down." He telephoned and

56

The Struggle of Jim Patros with Death

told them when the bus was leaving for Chester to come and get me, and when the driver came into the office he said, "Take this man home. Walk with him to his door."

The bus was full of different-different workers going home. In the bus I went to sleep and fell in the lap of an Italian fellow. The Italian said, "That's all right, my friend. That's all right."

When the driver woke me up the bus was empty. He walked with me to the door. The Greek doctor from Smyrna told the Greeks I was going to die, so a Greek fellow told the landlady I was dead. When she opened the door she didn't know if it was me or my spirit. You know Lazar? I was like Lazar. My face was all beard and bones. He told her I was dead. "You know that little fellow?" he said. "I buried him yesterday with my own hands. Jim Patros. Do not wait for him." She was very scared. So.

"Do not be scared, Mother," I said. "It is me. Jim Patros. I am not dead."

"My boy," she said. "How are you?"

"I am sick, Mother."

She took me to my room and put me in my bed. My eyes closed, but I could hear. "My boy," she said, "what can I do for you?"

"Mother," I said, "please go downstairs and get me some chicken broth."

So she went downstairs and got me a bowl of chicken broth. I drank the broth and closed my eyes to sleep. In the night something began to come up inside, very cold, so all night I didn't sleep.

Something told me to stay awake. In the morning the

57

landlady came and said, "My boy, tell me what I can do for you."

"Mother," I said, "please go downstairs and get me some chicken broth."

So she got me some chicken broth. About an hour later she came and said, "My boy, if there is anything in the world you want, please let me know."

She was crying. So.

"Mother," I said, "don't cry for me. If I am going to die, I'm going to die. We come into this world to live one life. Please get me some chicken broth."

Every hour until nighttime she brought me chicken broth.

In the night the Greek doctor and the government doctor came to look at me again. My eyes were closed, so they thought I couldn't hear. They said I was going to be dead by nine o'clock in the morning. "Well," I said to myself, "I don't know. Maybe the doctors know." When they went away the landlady came to me and began to cry.

"My boy, my boy," she said.

"Mother," I said, "it's all right. Don't cry for me."

She went away and after an hour she came back. "My boy," she said.

"Mother," I said, "don't waste your sleep for me. Go to bed. I heard what the doctors said. It's all right."

She went away but after an hour she came back. I could hear her walking around in the house.

"My boy," she said, "can I do anything for you?"

"It's all right, Mother," I said. "You go to sleep."

So this time she went to sleep. Inside my body the cold came up higher. I felt scared because I didn't know anything like that. I didn't know what it was. Then my nose began to bleed. At first I didn't know it was bleeding, but when I put my hand to my face my hand was warm and wet and I could smell the blood. It was coming fast. Under the bed I bent down for the pot and the blood dropped in for a long time. All the time it was falling, I began to feel better. Everything went away, came out of my nose with the blood. The room was dark but I knew I could see again. The cold was gone from the inside too. I was hungry but it was night-time, so I sat up in bed and waited for morning. In the morning I could hear the landlady walking past my door. She walked past many times, and then she stopped, so I said, "It's all right, Mother. I'm not dead. You can come in."

So she came in, but she was very scared. I showed her the blood. I was ashamed and I said, "Please forgive me, Mother. I couldn't help it."

"My boy," she said. "My boy. How are you? Are you all right?"

"I am very hungry, Mother."

She went downstairs and brought me some chicken broth. But I was very hungry, so she went upstairs and downstairs all morning bringing me chicken broth. When the doctors came I was sitting up in bed. They expected to see a dead body.

"What's this?" they said.

They examined me again, but now I was all right.

I didn't like them and they didn't like me.

The government doctor wrote down in his book and went away. The doctor from Smyrna walked around in the room.

59

Then he said, "I am going to ask you one question. Please tell me the truth."

"What is it?" I said.

"How old were you when you left the old country?"

"Seventeen," I said.

"All right," he said. "This is the question. How old were you when you began to wear shoes?"

"My father bought me shoes when I was three years old," I said. "But I threw them in the closet and ran into the hills in my bare feet. I didn't wear shoes as long as I was in Greece."

"That's the reason," the doctor said.

Then he went away.

You see, Jim said. From the earth to my feet came the strength of the old country. If I had worn shoes in the old country I would be dead now, not alive.

SAILING DOWN THE CHESA-PEAKE

"Come on, Nancy, put your best dress on!" the man on the radio sang. He had a plain nasal voice that was very appropriate for the song. He sounded silly, but the song itself had a strange enormous sadness.

"Dear Nancy," the boy in the hospital said. "Sweet Nancy."

It was Sunday now and it was still raining. It had been raining since Thursday night when he had come to the hospital. Now, in the East, where the man was singing, it was probably snowing. It was winter now, and all over the country, the streets were wet and cold, but on the radio, in a warm room somewhere in the East, the man was singing to Nancy. He was telling her to put on her best dress. That would be in a small town on the East coast somewhere, on the Chesapeake Bay. That would be a bay of blue, with a blue sky over it. Walking down the street of that small town twenty years ago, he was calling on the girl.

The young man looked up at the nurse, who wasn't like the girl of the song at all. She was the ugliest girl he had ever seen. "My luck," he said. "My miserable luck." The nurse was reading a big book. She'd been reading it since eight in the morning, and now it was late in the afternoon.

"What's it about?" he asked her.

Dear Baby

"Fellow named Rhett Butler," the nurse said.

"What about him?"

"It's about people down South."

"Tell me about them," he said.

"I'm not anywhere near started yet," the nurse said. "It's an awful long book."

"Well," he said, "I guess I'll never know then."

"You'll be all right."

"I'm all right *now*."

"Just rest."

"I'm resting all the time," he said. "I feel so at peace with the world. I'm living in my memories all the time now."

"How can you smile?" the nurse said.

"Why shouldn't I smile?"

"Aren't you sorry?"

"I am. I am *truly* sorry."

"Then how can you smile?"

"I don't know."

"Your poor mother," the nurse said.

"My poor mother," he said. "My poor, poor mother."

"That's more like it," the nurse said when she saw the tears in his eyes. They were the tears of a small boy who was truly sorry about what he'd done, and even though the nurse hadn't liked him from the beginning *because* of what he had done and the way he had talked before they had operated on him, she had felt forgiving.

"That's better," she said.

"I'm not crying about my mother," he said with anger. "I'm crying about my dirty filthy f——g luck."

62

The nurse got to her feet, trembling with rage.

"Sit down," he said. "Sit down and wait for me to die. That's what you're here for."

He smiled suddenly.

"Take it easy," he said. "I don't like people to be sorry for me, that's all. It's bad enough when I'm sorry for myself."

"You ought to be ashamed," the nurse said.

He laughed softly.

"Don't get sore," he said.

Two police came to ask if he had anything to give anybody.

"Nothing," he said.

It was a good thing everything was out in the open and he didn't have to protect anybody by keeping quiet. The two cops stood around, hating him, seeming to have something to say, not saying it, seeming to be on the verge of going, and then staying, as if they ought to shoot him. He turned their hatred back to them, smiling the way he knew they hated him for, only he wasn't acting, he wasn't trying to be tough, he was really sorry. He hadn't meant so much trouble. He hadn't meant so much trouble at all.

He was sorry about the poor police; about his friends; about his mother; and about himself. He was sorry about everybody, even the poor nurse. He was especially sorry about her.

The cops stood around, bringing to the small white room a smell of wet clothes, a smell of the world, that he was grateful for. They were good guys. He didn't hate them. He didn't hate anybody. Bad luck, that's all. Bad luck.

63

"What's your real name?" the one who hated him most said. He was big, Irish and rough, but probably underneath it all, kindly.

"Joe Renna."

"You're no Italian."

"You've got all my papers," he said. "My name's Joe Renna."

"You're no more Italian than I am," the cop said. "You're an American."

"Sure I'm an American," he said. "I was born on Columbus Avenue."

"What number?"

"I don't remember."

"Your mother or somebody will want to know about this," the cop said.

Tears came to his eyes again.

"They're all dead," he said.

"You've got somebody, haven't you?" the cop said.

The young man thought of naming the girl. She had surely read about it in the papers, but she hadn't even telephoned. It might be a nice joke to name her as the one to mourn him.

"I've got three hundred dollars in the bank," he said. "That ought to be enough for a funeral. You've got the book. If there's anything left over, give it to some boy in the street."

"How about your clothes?"

"I'll want to wear what's left of them. A good tailor can fix them up."

"How about the stuff where you live?"

"All I've got is what I had on me."

The cops went out, and once again he wanted to cry. It was no good to be going.

The nurse herself, after the cops had gone, turned on the radio.

All of a sudden the man on the radio began to sing about sailing down the Chesapeake, and the boy began to dwell in a time before he had been born, in a place he had never seen. He was walking down a summer street toward a girl he didn't know, and he didn't have much time. He stared at the nurse until she lifted her eyes from the pages of the book she was reading and *saw* him.

"Come here," he said.

The nurse got up and said, "What do you want?"

"I want you to know I love you," he said. (Come on, Nancy, put on your best dress and we'll go sailing down the Chesapeake. Oh, murder, murder.)

The nurse stood over him a moment and then put her hand on his forehead.

"Not there," he said. "On my mouth."

The nurse placed her hand over his mouth and the boy kissed it. (Oh, Nancy, Nancy.)

The radio singer was coming to the last chorus of the song.

"Bring your lips close to mine," he said.

The nurse bent over him, taking her lips so close that while he talked his lips touched hers.

"Just because you don't love me," he said, "don't ever think I don't love you. I love you more than any man has ever loved any woman."

Dear Baby

The singer came to the last chorus. The boy closed his eyes and began in a fury of trembling to sleep, standing cocky and confused in many places, turning, looking about, moving everywhere. Then, hurrying in a mob, he got to the little town on the East coast, twenty years ago, and went walking down the street under the blue sky, alive all over, his mouth full of thirst for cool water and for the taste of the lovely one, the whole world full of nothing but celebrations of love.

When his trembling stopped and his mouth fell open, the nurse hurried into the hall to fetch a doctor.

I KNOW YOU GOOD

One Saturday night in New York's Eastside a boy of thirteen named Irving went to his mother and said, "Ma, can I have a little money?"

"A little money?" his mother said. "How much money?"

"A dollar, Ma?"

"A dollar yet," the boy's mother said. "What for a dollar?"

"I need some new stuff at school," the boy said.

"New stuff?" his mother said. "What new stuff?"

"I need a new geography book, Ma."

"Geography?" his mother said. "What's geography?"

He was a good-looking young Jew, and it was summertime. He was getting interested in girls.

"Geography's all about places, Ma," he said.

"All about places," his mother said. "What places?"

"Australia, China, Ohio," the boy said.

"Australia, China, Ohio," the boy's mother said.

She gave him a very sharp look. "I know you good," she said.

She gave him ten cents.

Last Friday, in the San Joaquin valley, Yep and I got up at four in the morning and drove out to Riverdale to see how the barley was making out. We stopped along the highway every two or three miles to shoot at jack rabbits. The gun was a Winchester .22 repeater, borrowed from

Dear Baby

Yep's cousin Ara. I tried out the sight on a little bird that was perched on a telegraph wire, and dropped it. In no time at all I ended life in three of the lanky rodents, too. One of them I stopped while it was running. We enjoy this sort of thing. I think it's much less the lust to kill than the love of accuracy. I apologized to every rabbit of the desert that I killed. One, whose bowels had been spilled, sorrowed me deeply and made me ashamed of myself. I should have shot it in the head. The reason I didn't was that it was too far away.

I tried several times to get close enough to some crows that were in a couple of scrub trees, but as soon as I got too close they quietly took flight. (I know you good.)

A couple of miles north of Huron at eight in the morning we asked a boy on a threshing machine if he knew how we could reach Tuck's place. The boy had a mouthful of tobacco and stuttered. He was new in that region. He'd come down from the Tehachapi Mountains to drive the tractor that pulled the threshing machine around. Something had gone wrong with the machine, so that it cracked the barley. He was doing some work on the machine while someone was driving forty miles to Fresno for a new part. He said he disliked this new level country, preferred the mountains. I asked him where he was from originally, and he said Texas. He had punched cows in Old Mexico. His name was Will Young. He was twenty.

I shot two blackbirds that were in trees on an overflowing stream and the water carried their bodies away.

I went after some water birds of some sort. There were five of them. They were white and very beautiful from a distance standing in the swamp water, and even more beautiful in flight. While going near them I felt it would be wrong to shoot and kill one of them but at the same time I felt that I would try to do so. When we got about four hundred yards away from them, they all flew away quietly. Perhaps it was more than four hundred yards. It was too far away, at any rate, to shoot with accuracy.

Walking about out-of-doors, however, is an activity that pleases the heart. Five minutes ago, I decided to do it more often. (August 31, 1939. Delayed.)

THE NEW YEAR

It was raining, the third or fourth or fifth day of January, and I hadn't yet gotten over three or four things of December. I had money, I was bored, and what I had was either the flu or something like it. So I went into the restaurant, wobbling a little, still drunk from December, and frowning from the many sadnesses, irritations, and amazements of the year gone. In the back room where the bar is I found Tom, also drunk from December, and the two girls Mary and Emma.

It was ten minutes to twelve, midnight. The restaurant was empty except for the waiters. Even the back room was empty, except for Tom and Mary and Emma, and, of course, Joe, the Italian bar-boy, and Ben, the headwaiter.

It was a celebration. Tom was drunk but well-behaved, and the girls were drunk and full of high spirits. They screamed when they saw me, and Mary embraced and kissed me. Then Emma drew Mary away, and she embraced

69

Dear Baby

and kissed me. I kissed each of the girls as if only they knew the fable of the years lost, as if in all the world they were the only people who meant anything to me.

THE JOURNEY TO NEW YORK

The whole year he planned to go to New York, but didn't. He would be a little drunk as a rule whenever it occurred to him that he had planned to go and hadn't. He didn't even begin to lose faith in the journey, however, until one morning in August. He had been up all night and was waiting for a streetcar when day broke and made him wonder what had happened.

"New York?" he said. "—— New York. What's in New York?"

He turned, as if to someone with him, and said, "Which way did they go? You know. The years."

Then he gave the world a quiet cussing and decided all he wanted to do was sleep. —— everything.

After that he knew he wasn't going, and whenever he remembered New York it wasn't with any impulse to get there. "I'll go on rotting out here," he said.

He would get up around noon every day and go through the tiresome ritual of becoming alive again, shaving, bathing, putting on fresh clothes, and glancing with terrible distaste at the headline of the morning paper he had brought home with him. No matter how thoroughly he brushed his teeth and scraped his tongue, the taste he wakened with would stay foul until he had had two cups of coffee and a couple of cigarettes. He would feel better after that and would drink beer in the parlor until evening. He would have the blinds up for sunlight, if there was any, and sometimes he would sit at the piano and imagine he might get in the mood to play, but it always turned out that he didn't. Ordinarily, though, he wouldn't bother to notice the piano. Early in the evening he would take a streetcar to town and go to a quiet restaurant for the only meal of the day. It would be a very big one, and he would eat slowly, reading around in some pocket-size novel, or anthology of poems, or stories, or essays. From the restaurant he would go to a quiet bar and begin drinking. More often than not, people he had met somewhere would recognize him and come over to greet him. He would be polite but not enthusiastic, and they would know he wanted to be alone. After a moment they would leave, wondering what had come over him.

Drinking, he went to New York every night, and prowled through all the streets, looking for her, as if he didn't know she was not there, either.

FOO

"Now, about Chicago," he said. "If I go there, will I lose my hair?"

"Oh, you want to lose your hair?" the other said.

"No, I *don't* want to. That's what I want to know about Chicago. I've been thinking of going there. If I won't lose my hair, I'll go."

"Well," said the other, "take a look at my head."

He took off his hat and showed his head, which was bald, except around the sides.

71

Dear Baby

"That started," he said, "in Chicago." Pause. "I went there on business."

Another pause, while the man with hair regretted the other's misfortune.

"In 1928," the bald one said, "my hair started falling out the first day I was in Chicago."

"If you don't want to lose your hair," he said, "don't go to Chicago. But if you do, that's the place to go."

The man with hair, who was forty but much more youthful looking, almost boyish, an Italian from a family which had buried all its men with full heads of hair, whose own hair in fact was as thick as hair ever is, and probably couldn't have been torn out of his head, listened attentively and signified with a puckering of his lips, and a lifting of his eyebrows that he understood. The world, his expression seemed to say. What a place! If you go to Chicago, you lose your hair.

"I thought you might want to lose your hair," the other said.

"No," the Italian said with a smile. "I'll go somewhere else."

"You never know when it's liable to start falling out," the other said.

The Italian signified that he understood, perfectly.

"Nothing you can do about it, either," the other said. "I tried everything. It just kept right on falling out."

It was very hot. The two men had come to the back room of the cigar store because of the lower temperature there, and to have themselves a cool drink. The Italian was drinking Dr. Pepper, and the other, an American, was drinking

72

Coca-Cola. They had never met before and had hit upon Chicago as a subject of conversation more or less accidentally.

The American had said the heat was sultry—something like the heat of Chicago.

They finished their drinks, as they talked, put the empty bottles in the crates, and stood for a moment, cooling off.

The Italian was the first to go. Without a word, but not impolitely, he walked out to the street and the heat. The other lingered a moment and then followed the Italian.

The clerk behind the counter hadn't listened to their conversation, but when they were gone he said to himself, "Foo." It was a word he had been throwing about a good deal lately. He'd heard it from a tobacco salesman who'd come in one morning and said, " 'A stitch in foo saves foo.' "

"What's that?" the cigar-store clerk had asked.

"Foo, that's all," the salesman had said. "It's from the funnies. I got it from my kid. He's seven. Here's another, 'A foo and his money are soon parted.' "

"Say," the clerk had said, "that's good."

"No," the tobacco salesman had said, "not good, foo."

"O.K.," the clerk had said, "foo."

"Not O.K.," the salesman had said, "foo."

"Well, for crying out loud," the clerk had said, "at that rate you'd be saying 'foo' for everything."

"Foo," the salesman had said, meaning sure.

That's how it had started. The clerk had found the word useful, but lately it had begun to be a little difficult to control. Instead of saying thank you to a lady who had purchased a package of Herbert Raleigh cork tips he had said foo, and she had said I beg your pardon, and given him a very dirty foo. He meant look.

Well, foo to her. She was just a foo anyhow.

The world was foo, the human race was foo, love was foo, hate was foo, and above all things a man himself was foo.

MY WITNESS WITNESSETH

A number of things have been asking to get on paper, but they have been asking at unusual hours, so that by the time I have been ready to get them down on paper, they have been forgotten.

They ask, for instance, at two or three or four in the morning when I want to sleep.

Naturally, I refuse to get up and go to work, so by way of compromise I turn over, and in the morning remember that I knew the truth, but forgot it.

Last night, for instance, I knew the word: I knew it: and how smiling and kindly it was: how simple: how much a part of every man's heart: how miraculous and ordinary: how beautifully commonplace and, until last night, inexpressible.

An industrious writer, even in his youth, even in his old age, would have gotten up in the middle of the night with a vision like that, taken it by the tail, and out of it written a book.

But what do *I* do? I turn over and go to sleep.

Well, such is the life of the lazy writer. The fool puts sleep above revelation. In the morning he rises and seeks to write the foolish story of the foolish waste of everybody, naming, for argument's sake, the world as the criminal, naming the story The Criminal World, itemizing the misdemeanors, taking inventory of the mayhem, the arson, the theft, the false witness, the murder, the rape, the sodomy of it, or anything at all: telling a story that gets nowhere and means nothing.

My witness witnesseth that at the age of twelve I was a better writer than I am now at the age of thirty, except that I did not know how to write then, and now, knowing how, I must say I have lost the way, lost the vision, lost the world I knew must be made real, lost the realm of truth I knew was in myself, lost everything in fact except the few odd fragments of the commonplace world which so easily fit themselves into the so-easily written words.

"You write of yourself," they say—the critics, my relatives, my friends, and people who aren't friends at all. That is what they all say. "It reads well enough. It is all entertaining enough. It is all quite interesting, but it is always about yourself. Why is that?" What nonsense. Who am I to be myself?

The way I write now instead of the way I should have written, from the beginning, is unbelievable. And the millions of books, which were written by men at one time or another, which they sat down and deliberately wrote, which were printed and bound and for a time read—they are all the same: nothing, bloody nothing.

And nothing in the world is easier than to be a writer. Nothing is more stupidly flattering to one's self. Nothing is more pointless than to be another writer: anybody can be that: anybody at all. I can teach any man in the world to be that. That is a thing not worth teaching, I might say. And no one can blame me for the way I feel when the young men arrive and say with blushes or with firmness or with faith or with bitterness or with despair, "I want to write. I know I can write. How is it done?" I feel like a fool.

Anybody can be a writer. There is no middle-class boy in England or America who cannot be a writer. All he needs to do is work: just work: just muddle through.

I am sure of one thing: I am sure nothing is known. It is all to come when our eyes open; and something wonderful happens to our ears; and something incredible to our nostrils and lungs; and something to the pores all over us.

My witness witnesseth, but I wish to sleep, so by morningtime truth is lost, or at best in such a miserable state as this.

What can any writer born to write write when there isn't time enough in the years after twenty, or skill enough in the years before?

Even if you were born to write, even if you were born to look and see, listen and hear, feel and understand, sense and know, even then, by the time you're in command of the language, you're off in the jungle everybody's in, and you can write, but not really; you can write as they write and always have written; you can say everything that means nothing; you can do it expertly; you can make it a pleasure to read; but you can't carry them along to the living they want, you can't take them by the ear to life, you can't move the hour one second forward from where it was a million years ago; you can't say the word because you've forgotten it; you can't do anything but wait, the same as the others— making the pathetic stab at living the others are making, never coming to life, arriving dead from the dead, out of

77

death creating the new dead, putting them on their feet, putting them into the streets, turning them loose into the mouse-trap world.

This is most certainly a sad transcript of the things that have been asking to get down on paper, but it is certainly the best I can do with the language I know, the body I inhabit, the mind I tried to educate. This is most certainly not the word. I, Saroyan, am most certainly not the man to say the word, but I know it is there, waiting to be said, and I hope to God somebody will do me a favor and say it. I'm too lazy.

THE FLASHLIGHT

Next to having a revolver (which of course you could never get; which you would never really *want;* which, nevertheless, it was always pleasant to imagine you wanted more than anything else in the world), having a flashlight was a wonderful thing.

You could never have a revolver because you might make a mistake with it and kill a friend instead of Mr. Davis, the principal of Emerson School. You might not be accurate with the thing and you might shoot off somebody's nose. Somebody nice, standing on the corner, at high noon, with his hand over where his nose had been, and your heart full of regret, and your mouth trying to say, "Honest, Mr. Wheeler, I didn't mean to shoot your nose off. I was shooting at that chicken-hawk flying over the roof of the Republican Building. I'm sorry, Mr. Wheeler. I apologize."

Or you might get bawled up, trying to take a quick second shot at the circling chicken-hawk, turn quickly, and shoot off your own nose.

It was the same with a horse, too.

Unpredictable.

A flashlight was another story.

Your sick cousin Joe's real name was Hovsep. Hovsep is Joseph in Armenian. Like yourself, Joe was eleven years old, only funnier. A month and a half younger, too. Which means that—well, you were first. You were ahead of him. You arrived a month and a half before he did.

Dear Baby

So you went in and asked his mother how he was and tears came to her eyes, and she said, "I don't know. The doctor's with him."

You went out to the street, into the darkness of November, and began to walk home. You wished you had the revolver and the horse, so you could jump on the horse and go galloping over the streets, and draw the revolver, and do something swift and reckless to make Joe get better.

The whole thing was a mistake. Joe had no business being sick with the flu, and if he died—well, by God, you'd get even. "If Joe dies," you said on the way home, "you'll get yours." It was a clear cold night and it was the greatest time in the world to be alive, with many wonderful years of adventure ahead.

You were too busy being sore about Joe to remember how scared you were of the dark, and then all of a sudden you remembered. For a minute you were real scared, and then you pressed your thumb down on the button of the flashlight, and the light went on, and you weren't scared any more. So you flashed the light around; to the ground; up into the branches of trees; left and right; north and south. And then suddenly, as you walked, it was all over, Joe was dead, you were walking down the street alone, the years were gone, it was a night in November again many years later, and you were still sore and you still couldn't believe it. You flashed the light to the trunk of a tree and said, "Joe?" But nobody was there. And a moment later you turned the light to the dark steps of a porch, thinking he might be sitting there, and you said, "Joe?" But he wasn't there, either.

The Flashlight

The next day you couldn't wait to run over to Joe's during lunch hour. When the noon bell rang, you jumped out of your desk, got to the door first, got out of the building first, and began running up L Street, down San Benito Avenue, until you got tired and couldn't run any more. "Please," you said. "Please don't let Joe die." You got out the flashlight and turned it on, but the daylight was brighter than the light of the flashlight, and you could see everything, so what good was a flashlight now? You kept hurrying and flashing the light at everything, as if it were night, as if Joe was in the last night of life, and you were looking for him, and you kept asking the question: "Joe?"

At last you got to the house and stood on the sidewalk and looked at it. Was it a house that had a dead boy in it named Joe? Was it a house full of the amazed, sorrowing mothers and fathers, grandmothers and grandfathers, great-grandmothers and great-grandfathers of Joe Hagopian, the eleven-year-old American whose family arrived seventeen years ago from Bitlis? Did the house contain the living and the dead of a tribe just cheated of its son?

You went to the back door, quietly into the kitchen, and saw his mother, and you knew from her face that the light from the flashlight had found God's heart in the darkness of the November night, and in the brightness of the November day, and you knew Joe was alive, with the heart of God beating in him. And you knew that that great heart would go on beating in him all the years that had roared by your ears the night before. You knew the dead grandmothers and grandfathers were all smiling, and you didn't say anything. You just looked up at Joe's mother and smiled.

"He's all right now," she said. "He'll be up in a few days. Come back after school. Maybe he'll be awake."

"Sure," you said. "Here, when he wakes up, give him this flashlight. He can flash it on in the night at the walls and the ceiling. Mighty fine invention."

HOW IT IS TO BE

When George Gershwin died, I believed I ought to have an X-ray picture taken of my head, but the doctor told me it wouldn't be necessary.

"It's something we don't know anything about," he said. "All we know is that there are two kinds of growths, benign and malignant. We don't know why there is either. That's the part you're supposed to find out about."

"Me?" I said. "What do you mean, *me?*"

"I mean," he said, "your guess is as good as anybody's, maybe better."

"Thanks," I said, "but how about these pains in my head every once in a while?"

"Well," he said, "how about the pains in my head every once in a while? Get the idea? It's nothing, or at any rate nothing that isn't a natural or at least an inevitable part of living."

"That's different," I said. "Just so everybody has them. Just so it's not because I'm a writer."

"It's not because you're a writer," he said. "It's because you're dying, so forget it, because everybody's dying."

"My God," I said, "is that true?"

"You know it is," he said. "You know better than I do that it's true. None of us is more than a minute from death at any time. You know that. Absence of oxygen and hydrogen, as when a man is drowning, can carry us out in almost no time at all. Loss of relationship, equilibrium, or position, as when a man is falling, can do it in two or three seconds. Collision, as when a man is carried swiftly to an object composed of firmer substance than himself, can do it instantaneously. These are the accidental and more violent passages, but even normally none of us is more than a minute from death."

So I decided to ignore the pains in my head.

Even so, that was the saddest news I'd heard in years because one night in New York I'd met him and talked to him and he'd played the piano for a couple of hours. He was only a boy. Nobody wants anybody like that to die at the age of thirty-five or thirty-six. Nobody wants anybody who can hear music to die while he's still a boy. I talked to Sibelius once. That's *how* we want it to be. Sibelius was close to seventy.

I was in my home town when I heard about it. One of my cousins told me about it. He came over to my grandmother's in his Chevrolet roadster and we started driving to Kingsburg. When we got out on the highway near Malaga he turned on the radio. There was an orchestra swinging around, and all of a sudden my cousin remembered.

"Gershwin's dead," he said.

Well, all he had to do was say it and I knew it was true. If my cousin said it, it was true. I couldn't believe it, but I knew it was true. Remembering Gershwin in New York I believed my cousin when he said Gershwin was dead. By God, it was true. There it was. He was dead. I looked at the grapevines in the beautiful light, the lovely trees, and the quiet roads.

"Did you know him?" my cousin said.

"I met him one night in New York," I said. "It was a big party and there were a lot of people and everybody was drinking and talking, but I guess I knew him."

We went out to the vineyard in Kingsburg and saw the vines and the grapes on them.

Then we went back to my grandmother's and had lunch: grape leaves wrapped around lamb and rice, Armenian bread and cheese, and cold watermelon. Then we drove out to the park and I kept looking at everything. I kept wondering how it is to *be*. How it *is*. How incredible and splendid it is. How strange and mournful and fine: having all the quiet things that were painted by great men who painted when *they* wanted to know how it is: the still-lifes, the forms of the quiet things, the pear, the peach, the cluster of grapes, the fish on the plate, the loaf of bread, the bottle of wine, the real things, in light. How magnificent and good and mysterious the living things are that all men have loved.

At two in the morning that night I took the train for San Francisco and went on looking at everything: the darkness of the landscape and the sky, waiting for the coming of light, the wan arrival of morning, the coming up of the sun, lighting up the world we have made, the ugly lovely world we have put on the earth, the railroads and industrial buildings, and the quiet sorrowing dwellings of poor people. I dreamed all night of how it is.

I'll try to tell you how it is. If I can remember, I'll go to all the places I have gone to by train or ship, and if I can remember what happened, I'll tell you, because if the pains in my head aren't because I'm a writer, what it is to me is what it is to you, and what it is to you is what it is to all the others who are still alive, who have not yet traveled, in wars or accidents or disease to the other side. If I can keep from trying to say everything at once, I'll tell you how it is, or at least give you an idea.

I'll go back to the beginning, if I can. That's got to be, otherwise it won't be whole. The beginning is when *you* begin, and that isn't when you're born, except in a matter-of-fact statistical way. When you're born is the beginning all right, but not the one I'm thinking about. The beginning I mean is the one when you yourself *look* and for the first time *see*.

The beginning I mean is when you come out of the dream being dreamed by the universe and feel the lonely, fierce glory of being, of being out of emptiness, of being related to, and a part of, the great source of energy, of being an entity, whole and perishable, benign and malignant.

The beginning I mean is when you know the difference between what men pretend to be and what they are: not anything but visitors of the world, borrowers of time, coming and going. Not possessors of anything but the privilege of inhabiting substance and enduring time. Men are miraculously living things, never more than a day from death, never far from glory, and as long as they live children, because living is in its infancy. Men who travel the last moment to death at the age of seventy, or eighty, or ninety, travel as children. They go as they came, helplessly.

Let them have been great in the eyes of their fellows, or

small, or unknown, or in the eyes of God let them have been noble and good and true, men, when they travel that last moment, go as men *coming* here travel the *first* moment. Those moments, that of coming to this place and that of leaving it, are the moments of mystery and miracle, benign and, if we choose to put it the other way, malignant, although coming is no more benign than going is malignant. Each is simultaneously malignant and benign.

They are always *together*, except for climate, and light, and the fragments of time each man knows that are of glory, of reaching destination in the opposite of one's kind. Benign and malignant are one in the living, in all things, except for these moments when the moving of time is halted by the infinite rise of heart, the immeasurable lift of spirit, the momentarily unending expansion of truth seeking truth, and finding it.

This is a suggestion of how it is, a suggestion of how *some* of it is. The parts are so numerous and so variable that no man may say how *all* of it is. Even for himself no man, no child here, great or small, or in the eyes of God noble and true, may know how *all* of it is, or even how all of it *may* be. It may be for now, as the ballad goes, or it may be for ever. For now or for ever, no man may know.

The evening of that day, in my home town, my cousin and I rode around the Sunday streets and suddenly saw one of the opposite of our kind, born in that place, walking through the evening, as lovely as a cluster of grapes. My cousin roared. He drove the roadster up and down the street, keeping the girl in sight, roaring with delight and adoration, slapping the side of his head with sorrow, groaning in Armenian, and saying in English, "Oh, my God."

The girl was no more than sixteen or seventeen, or maybe no more than fourteen or fifteen, but as lovely as all young things of our earth are, as charged with grace and proportion as all things coming into this life are: the coming of day, fruit to the bough, sea to the shore, humor to the heart. And with my cousin, I was smitten with that grief which comes from delight and adoration of substance so lovely it is holy, though it be possessed by the daughter of a drunkard or an idiot or any man, great or small. My cousin and I saw mortal loveliness, and when it disappeared into a hovel, on a desolate street by a railroad track, my cousin, still groaning, looked about furiously and shouted, "Let's go get a root beer."

We drove to a place on Ventura Avenue and had two of them. Then we drove out to his house. A dozen of us, all from the same sources, sat around and talked. The older ones remembered the old country and those who had died; the early days in this country, and how beautiful everything had been, how beautiful and different, and the same. The hard times and the times when one of us, still alive, was on his way to the last moment and the others prayed and swore and finally the one who was journeying turned and came back to us and at last all the others fell down and slept and in the morning the journeyer slept peacefully and a week later, or two or three, was back with us again, still one of us, talking with us, aged three or twenty, or forty, and laughed with us, and we were together still and there would be tables together still, food and drink together, seasons together still, and light in the world still. We talked of the dead as if they were not dead, as if the years had not gone by, as if Dikran was among us still, brilliant and swift and full of comedy, roaring with laughter, hugging the children of his sisters, bringing them gifts. We talked of Hovagim and his old rattletrap Buick and his ferocious anger when somebody was unkind or a liar, his fury one day when a neighbor lied to him, and how he lifted the neighbor's Ford and tipped it over on its side and shouted, "There! Now lie some more!" And all of us roared with laughter.

Later that night my cousin and I drove to town again and went to a bar.

"Do you remember the men they were talking about?" my cousin asked.

"A few of them I remember," I said. "Some were before my time, but I remember Hovagim. He took me and my brother out to his vineyard once in his rattletrap Buick. He took us hunting and played Armenian records on his old phonograph, and tears came down his eyes. He used to bring us grapes and peaches and watermelons. I remember this man, but I don't remember Dikran. I remember *hearing* about him from his sister, my mother, and from his mother, our grandmother. I like him. He seems to have been a solemn man, even though he was always comical."

We went to the Basque saloon on Tulare Street. There was a nickel-in-the-slot phonograph there and for two hours we sat around drinking Scotch and listening to Spanish tangoes and love songs. It was a good place. It was one of the best places of drinking I ever drank in, and I kept thinking of the night in New York when I met George Gershwin and he told me how it was with him when he composed.

Drinking, I knew how it is, but I couldn't say. It's the way nobody knows. He had journeyed past the last moment, but he was with us still because while he possessed substance he journeyed back and forth, into the darkness and back to the light, looking and listening, going into the region just beyond all of us, and coming back. I knew it was *that* way. But for the grace of God any of us is to be dead before we have come or gone, before we have begun, before we have reached any moment to remember, we are earth again, or rock, or nothing.

On the train going home I was a sad Armenian, as they say of Indians. It wasn't because Brahms had died, or Bach, or any of the others, Renoir, or Goya, or Dostoyevsky, or Dickens, or Robert Burns, or Byron, or Daniel Boone, or Tolstoy, or Andrew Jackson, or Mark Twain, or any of the others we love. It was because that's how it is, malignant and benign, by the grace of God, by the mercy of God.

MR. FLEMING AND THE
SEVEN WONDERS OF
THE WORLD

I have seen the seven wonders of the world, and if there is an eighth, I have seen it, and if a ninth, it. I have strolled through the public parks of every civilized and un-civilized country in the world. I have slept in the finest beds of the finest hotels in the best cities of the best continents. I have guzzled the choicest juices of the choicest grapes, dined on fowl and fish, beef and lamb. I have lolled through long afternoons in the gardens of the richest people on earth, sipping green tea, reading cheap novels, and smoking expensive cigars. I have walked through moonlight with society women, Woolworth salesgirls, and movie actresses. I have played poker with the Prince of Wales, billiards with the Countess of Strasbourg, and post office with the widow of the wealthiest cattleman in Texas, and now this old ave-nue of aches has got me.

Seven of the wonders I have seen, but the only place is Beale Street.

There are honest men here, and skilled pickpockets. Liv-ing doesn't end until somebody gets killed.

I have had little public schooling, but I have done a lot of walking around. I have scrambled upstairs, thinking to reach God, or heaven, or the lost earth, and I have reached nothing, or nothing more than a small and desolate room, thick with the stench of female sweat and the stare of professional evil. I have fallen downstairs, drunk and delirious, and I have busted my legs and my arms, my head and my heart.

I am weary of longing, but I cannot stop. It is in my family to be this way, and even here, on this street, the old heart aches for the illuminated city, the old blood wails for the greater nation.

I remember that the tree trembled in the wind, the bird flew south, and the leaves fell. I sat there all day, remembering the face of Leonora, chanting the devotional exercises of Christians of various denominations: nothing but love (baby): I got a woman crazy for me: she's funny that way. O Katerina my Katerina: honey, take a look at me: it's the last you're going to get, you see: I dreamt that I held you.

Beale Street, Michigan Boulevard, Broadway, The Strand, and Piccadilly.

I saw her in the meadow, and I said, "O lovely. Leah, O Leah." But she said no word.

I stood alone on a corner in Texas, and up the street tripped the lady with the feathered hat. "Greetings," I said.

Texas Trixie, the phonograph crying, "I hate to see that evening sun go down." (Blind man on the corner singing Song of Songs.)

Let them be turned backward and put to confusion that desire my hurt.

In the room at the Rex Hotel I said to her, "Woman, I have brought you my heart on a cafeteria tray, my money on a copy of *True Confessions*. What is your name?"

PASSENGERS TO EUROPE

Joe Nikcik, Chicago Croatian on the way home to his eighty-eight-year-old mother in Zagreb, third-class *Normandie*, four o'clock in the morning, rough sea, first day out:

"Mr. William, I been lying down not sleeping. Twenty-seven year ago I come to America. Now I go back to see my moder before she die."

He begins to cry like a boy of eight crying. Joe is a little over fifty; about six feet three; broad; and about two hundred and thirty pounds in weight.

The high school teacher who shares the four-man cabin and spends all his time playing bridge is gone. He used to be an infant prodigy. The Norwegian boy on his way home to Bergen is out after the girls, singing, "Chiu, chiu, to Broadway, foo Cincinnati," which leaves Joe and the writer.

Joe cries without shame. The light is dim, the boat is rolling from one side to the other, the writer is drunk, so it's all right, it's all right for Joe to cry.

The Norwegian boy comes to the cabin, drunk and full of laughter because although he got to the door of her cabin, and although he didn't like her in the first place, she drove him away as if she were the girl with the golden hair in the opera. "Come along," he told her. "Come along —chiu, chiu, to Broadway."

93

Dear Baby

"I shall ring for the steward," she said. "You must go away."

"Ring for Jesus," the boy told her.

The Norwegian boy tells the whole story. Joe listens carefully, laughing at the boy—twenty-two years old—seven months from home, the framed photograph of his girl always near—a most beautiful girl, truly the one of the golden hair in the opera. He runs into a wretch of a woman who is lonely and eager for adventure, and being drunk, he is willing to be everything for her, but at the door of her cabin she threatens to ring for the steward.

"Chiu, chiu, to Broadway," the boy sings. "You want a drink, Joe?"

"I don't mind if I do," the Croatian says and takes a swig from the bottle which the boy always keeps with him.

"What you been doing?" Joe says, as if the boy hadn't been telling him.

The Norwegian himself sees a new dimension of inquiry in this question and very casually says, "Just killing a little time, Joe." He sits down very somberly and studies the floor.

Suddenly the song reaches the part he cannot hum inwardly, so he busts out with, "Hold tight, hold tight—hold tight, hold tight, frrrrrrnakasaki, want some sea food, maaama."

He grows somber again. He turns, looks at the framed picture of his girl, kisses the glass, looks at Joe, kisses the glass again, busts out laughing, and then remembering the woman, says, "I just wanted to make her happy."

"Who was the woman?" Joe says.

94

"I won't tell," the boy says. "She's *so* ugly."

"Ha ha ha," Joe says.

The boy goes away to kill some more time, and in three minutes Joe is crying again.

This happened in June of 1939, when there was no war.

THE DECLARATION OF WAR

On September the third, 1939, a boy by the name of John came running into the barber shop on Moraga Avenue where I was getting a haircut.

"War's been declared in Europe," he said.

Mr. Tagalavia dropped the comb from one hand and the scissors from the other.

"You get out of this shop," he said. "I told you before."

"What's your name?" I said to the young man.

"John," he said.

"How old are you?" I said.

"Eleven," John said.

"You get out of this shop," Mr. Tagalavia said.

I was under the impression that Mr. Tagalavia was talking to John, but apparently he wasn't. He was talking to me. He wasn't talking to *himself*.

John had left the shop.

The barber untied his apron and threw it aside.

"Who?" I said.

"You," Mr. Tagalavia said.

"Why?"

"I try to run a respectable barber shop."

"I'm respectable."

"You talked to that foolish boy," the barber said. "I don't want people like you to come to my shop."

"He didn't *seem* foolish," I said.

The Declaration of War

"He is a foolish, foolish boy," the barber said. "I don't want foolish people to come here."

"I suppose it *was* a little foolish of me to ask the boy his name," I said. "I'm sorry about that. I'm a writer, you see, and I'm *always* asking people questions. I apologize. Please finish my haircut."

"No," the barber said. "That's all."

I got out of the chair and examined my head. My haircut was less than half finished. The shape of my head wasn't exactly what it might be, but I could always walk three or four blocks and have the job finished by an ordinary barber. I put on my tie and coat.

"Excuse me," I said. "How much do I owe you?"

"Nothing," the barber said. "I don't want money from people like you. If I starve—if my family starves—all right. No money from foolish people."

"I'm sorry," I said, "but I believe I owe you *something*. How about thirty-five cents?"

"Not a penny," the barber said. "Please go away. I will make a present of the haircut to you. I *give* to people. I do not take. I am a man, not a fool."

I suppose I should have left the shop at this point, but I felt quite sure that what he *really* wanted to do was talk.

I have a power of understanding which is greater than the average, and at times uncanny. I sense certain things which other people, for one reason or another, are unable to sense.

(Sometimes what I sense is wrong and gets me in trouble, but I usually manage to get out of it. A kind word. A friendly tone of voice. A worldly attitude about such things.

Dear Baby

We are all brothers. The end is death for each of us. Let us love one another and try not to get excited.)

I sensed now that the barber was troubled or irritated; that he wished to speak and be heard; that, in fact, unless I missed my guess, his message was for *the world*. Traveling thousands of miles he could not have found anyone more prepared to listen to the message or to relay it to the world.

"Cigarette?" I said.

"I don't want anything," the barber said.

"Can I help you with the towels?"

"You get out of my shop."

Here, obviously, was an equal if I had ever encountered one. I have at times been spoken of by certain women who follow the course of contemporary literature as enigmatic and unpredictable, but after all I am a writer. One expects a writer to be impressive along the lines of enigma and so on, but with barbers one usually expects a haircut or a shave or both, along with a little polite conversation, and nothing more. Women who have time to read are likely to believe that it is natural for a writer to have certain little idiosyncrasies, but perhaps the only man in the world who can allow a *barber* similar privileges is a writer.

There is little pride in writers. They know they are human and shall some day die and be forgotten. We come, we go, and we are forgotten. Knowing all this a writer is gentle and kindly where another man is severe and unkind.

I decided to offer the barber the *full* cost of a haircut. Sixty-five cents, instead of thirty-five. A man can always get a haircut. There are more important things than making sure one has not been swindled.

The Declaration of War

"Excuse me," I said. "I don't think it's fair to you for me not to pay. It's true that you haven't finished my haircut, but perhaps some other day. I live near by. We shall be seeing more of one another."

"You get out of my shop," the barber said. "I don't want people like you to come here. Don't come back. I have no time."

"What do you mean, people like me? I am a writer."

"I don't care what you are," Mr. Tagalavia said. "You talked to that foolish boy."

"A few words," I said. "I had no idea it would displease you. He seemed excited and eager to be recognized by someone."

"He is a foolish, foolish boy," the barber said.

"Why do you say that?" I said. "He seemed sincere enough."

"Why do I say that!" the barber said. "Because he *is* foolish. Every day now for six days he has been running into my shop and shouting, War! War! War!"

"I don't understand," I said.

"You don't understand!" the barber said. "War! I don't know who you are, but let me tell you something."

"My name is Donald Kennebec," I said. "You may have heard of me."

"My name is Nick Tagalavia," the barber said. "I have never heard of you."

He paused and looked me in the eye.

"War?" he said.

"Yes," I said.

"You are a fool," the barber said. "Let me tell you something," he went on. "There is no war! I am a barber. I do not like people who are foolish. The whole thing is a trick. They want to see if the people are still foolish. They *are*. The people are more foolish now than ever. The boy comes running in here and says, 'War's been declared in Europe,' and you talk to him. You encourage him. Pretty soon he believes everything, like you."

The barber paused and looked at me very closely again. I took off my hat, so he could see how far he had gone with the haircut, and how much he had left unfinished.

"What do you write?" he said.

"Memoirs," I said.

"You are a fool," the barber said. "Why do you encourage the boy? He's going to have trouble enough without wars. Why do you say, 'How old are you'?"

"I thought he was rather bright," I said. "I just wanted him to know I was aware of it."

"I don't want people like you to come to my shop," the barber said.

"People like me?" I said. "I *hate* war."

"Shut up," the barber said. "The world is full of fools like you. You hate war, but in Europe there *is* a war?"

The implication here was a little too fantastic.

"Excuse me," I said. "*I* didn't start the war."

"You hate war," the barber said again. "They tell you there's a war in Europe, so you believe there's a war in Europe."

"I have no reason to believe there's peace in Europe," I said.

"You hate war," he said. "The paper comes out with the

headline War. The boy comes running into the shop. War. You come in for a haircut. War. Everybody believes. The world is full of fools. How did you lose your hair?"

"Fever," I said.

"Fever!" the barber said. "You lost your hair because you're a fool. Electric clippers. Comb. Scissors. You've got no hair to cut. The whole thing is a trick. I don't want any more fools to come here and make me nervous. There is no war."

I had been right in sensing that the barber had had something to say and had wanted someone to say it to. I was quite pleased.

"You are a remarkable man," I said.

"Don't talk," the barber shouted. "I'm no foolish boy of eleven. I'm fifty-nine years old. I am a remarkable man! Newspapers. Maps. You've got no hair on your head. What am I supposed to cut? The boy comes running in. You can't sit still. 'War is declared in Europe,' he says. 'What's your name? How old are you?' What's the matter? Are you crazy?"

"I didn't mean to upset you," I said. "Let me pay you."

"Never," the barber said. "I don't want anything. That's no haircut. Not a penny. If a man with a head of hair comes in here and sits down, I will take the electric clippers and give him a haircut. The hair falls down on the floor. No trouble. No excitement. No foolishness. He gets out of the chair. His head is in good shape. Ears feel fine. Sixty-five cents. Thank you. Good-bye. The boy comes running in. I say, 'Get out of my shop.' The boy runs out. No trouble."

"*Other* barbers give me haircuts," I said.

Dear Baby

"All right," he said. "Go to other barbers. Please go to other barbers. Remember one thing. There is no war. Don't go around spreading propaganda."

I was now satisfied that I had successfully gotten to the bottom of the man's irritation, and had obtained fresh and original material for a new memoir, so without another word, I sauntered out of the shop and down the street.

I feel that I have effectively utilized the material; that I have shaped it into a work which, if anything, will enhance my already considerable fame.

HIGHWAY AMERICA

I have been to Secaucus. I have crossed the Passaic.

That was the day after I bought the car. That was that rainy Sunday. I remember a lot of churches in one of those Jersey towns. I remember a couple of trees and a lot of lawn somewhere. I remember rain and a Greek or Roman Catholic Sunday service of some kind over the radio, with no word known, but good voices and considerable chanting. Later the radio broke.

What's the use being a writer if you aren't going to have a car and see the United States? Where does it ever get you? My cousin drove for me. He is a natural-born comedian. Another thing about him that's fine is that he talks Armenian. That's a great funny language. American is another great funny language, and when you put the two together you get something that's really casual.

The hardest thing of all is to get out of town. It's worth it, though. Down Fifth Avenue to the Holland Tunnel into Jersey and onto Pulaski Skyway. Pulaski was a Pole who fought the red-coats, I think. On highway Nine past the Newark Airport onto 22. Right on down to Galloping Hill Park and onto 29, to Watchung Mountain, Copper Hill, Ringoes, New Hope. Well, look at that. Lahaska. 202 now. Paoli and the freckle-faced, ripe and bursting beauty in the highway restaurant bringing the spare ribs and sauerkraut to the swing of nickel-in-the-slot. A couple of the boys from Fresno, California. Arminimums, my cousin explains. Lost—Westchester County. This is a county of some social importance, even though we're off the road, I inform my cousin. In Armenian he makes appropriate reply by word and gesture, and we recover the road over 322 at Downington. Black Horse, Paradise, Bird-in-Hand. People have no idea how wonderful they are. And as for you, child, you are an angel. She waved. The Delaware! Isn't there something important about this river? He wants to know isn't there something important about the Delaware. Listen, boy, Washington *crossed* the Delaware.

We cross the Susquehanna.

Just outside Gettysburg we bought three old rifles and one old little revolver that the girl wanted $14 for that I couldn't afford which she said another man bought one just like it only a month ago.

"Who was he?" I said.

"He was a stranger," she said.

Now about this little revolver I bought for a dollar and a half. Well, it's hard to say, but it seems they were playing cards and the man who had this gun concealed in his upper left-hand vest-pocket suspected another man of cheating. He drew this gun, fired it, and stung the other man in the cheek. The other man said ouch and killed the man who, probably sixty-seven years ago, owned my gun.

We had a few minutes in Maryland. "This is Mencken's state," I said, and together we sang "Maryland, My Maryland." "That's Wagner," my cousin said. Thus, we crashed headlong into Virginia and new adventure. We saw pigs on the side of the road looking like dogs, red and furry. Off the highway a mile to the Shenandoah Caverns. "We'll see these awful wonders of the world if it costs us fifty cents each," my cousin said. "A dollar sixty-five each," the man said. "We'd see it," I said, "if it was a dollar seventy, but first let us eat." The waitress was also the cook. "Those pigs," I said. "They look like dogs. What are they called?" "Piggies," she said. We saw the caves. Forty or fifty million years old, just like the dirt upstairs. We got through an hour-and-a-half lecture tour in ten minutes, instructing the guide along the way.

Little Rock, Malvern, Arkadelphia, Texarkana, and then Texas. You forget a lot. It's a big country. It's beautiful. Big Spring for sleep. Rain all the way in. Through Fort Worth. Nine cars, three trucks, tipped over in the mud on the side of the highway. We got to El Paso around six-thirty the next day. Mexican supper. Mexican music on the phonograph. Across the border to Juarez. Entering Juarez the Mexican Customs man arrived and said:

"Wharr gee wanna go?"

"Juarez."

"Wharr gee wanna do?"

"Drive around."

"Where gee wanna drive around?"

"Just around around."

"Where gee wanna drive around around?"

"Just around around around."

"Nineteen cents please," he said, letting us into Old Mexico.

On into New Mexico. The highway dips every half mile. Dips are cheaper than bridges. Into Arizona. Safford for

105

the night. In Arizona we improvised on themes of Armenian folk music, and finally put words to something called Automobile, Automobile. This was sad, but wonderful, going ninety miles an hour and looking. The hills, the valleys, the streams, the trees, the rocks, the towns, the people. The heart chanting, *"Aye vakh!"*

After we forgot the song of the automobile, we put a few simple American words to an Armenian theme of music. The fellow says, "Come on to my house. I'm gonna give you candy."

Down the American highway into the valley of home. "Home," my cousin says. In the valley he busts out laughing. "Hey, look. The vines." (I'm looking. Don't worry. I'm looking.)

It's a beautiful country, but the most beautiful thing about it is that it's just like every country in the world—on account of the people, most likely.

MY HOME, MY HOME

Of the unchanging things, the town in which you first saw the light is one of the most unchanging. It is always a place of monotony but at the same time, as you grow, change, go away, remember, return, and go away again, it is one of the most inexhaustibly rich places. And yet what it is is so nearly nothing, except for the dull, drab, lonely, lost objects of it, that you never know, each time you return to it, what it is that holds you so strongly to it.

What is it but an ordinary American town, no different from ten thousand others, where thirty million others were once born and where once they knew childhood and youth, and went away or stayed?

What is it more than a place where two or three dozen rested one day of one year and stayed, and others came, and stayed, and still others came out of their staying?

What is it more than two depots, one on each side of town, east and west, the city in between, the streets and houses all around, the dwellers never out of hearing of the trains coming and going?

What is it more than the beginning of the world, with winter coming?

Is it anything more than waking one morning and knowing presence in this place?

Or more than sitting at a desk at school and wishing to learn from the simplest lesson of arithmetic what *all* of it is, who all of them are?

Dear Baby

Is it ever a place more than where, not in dream, the streets occurred and yourself came about in them, walking?

Is it anything more than longing, summer and winter? Loneliness you do not know shall never end?

Is it anything more than beholding beauty in the face of a small girl and adoring it and not knowing that never shall the light of that face go out of your sleep?

Is the small town a place, truly, of the world, or is it no more than something out of a boy's dreaming? Out of his love of all things not of death made? All things somewhere beyond the dust, rust, and decay, beyond the top, beyond all sides, beyond bottom: outside, around, over, under, within?

Is it a boy's knowing that, although this is a place of sorrowed trying, of sorrowful men trying for the best, it is also a place where in the midst of things seen and men known moves the race that never was born, and within the crying grief of its streets and structures is the whole towering world which almost came to be? To his nostrils just beyond the stench of sweat and rot, the holy scent of all things with only loveliness in them and no death? To his ears, the stillness of silence staying within and around all things? The soft, listening silence of the continuous beginning?

Once again I am back in my home town. Last night I learned that a great part of what this town is, wherever I go: is the nighttime sky: clear, sudden, and infinitely spacious.

Early this morning I walked to town down Ventura Avenue over streets I walked twenty years ago. I found nothing changed but a few signs on a few buildings, a few trees lost, a few new ones come, a few grown greater, a house fallen into disrepair but still inhabited, the porch in decay. The silence is the same, and it is broken the same as twenty years ago, by the coming and going of trains.

From Ventura Avenue to Tulare Street I walked on the Santa Fé railroad tracks, and from the north going south came the freight train. When it reached me I couldn't believe the years had gone, and I knew a man will go out of this world without ever finding that largeness and wholeness in the living and in himself which was the cause of all his longing when he was no more than ten years old.

While the train was going by, I knew that a man will go away without ever having reached anywhere, and never will the image of loveliness just beyond all things, all ends and edges, over and above and within, cease to be in his sleep until he is truly one who is no longer alive, and no longer able to sleep at all.

THE GRAPES

These were the earliest grapes of the year, excepting the very earliest ones from Imperial Valley. On the vines the grapes might not be ripe enough in the morning, but by three in the afternoon they would be all right, so the Mexicans and Filipinos and Oklahomans would cut the bunches from the vines and put them in boxes, and seven days later the grapes would be in New York. They would ripen in six hours of that kind of heat and their color would change from a soft transparent green to a light brown, and then the government inspector would take a half-dozen bunches and mash them and test them for sugar. They would be sweet enough, or so close to it that he wouldn't make any trouble. A new inspector would always make trouble, or start to, but an old one would let the grapes go into the refrigerator car, just so they were close to the mark. The grapes would be packed in crates, about twenty-eight pounds to a crate, although some shippers would pack the crates heavy and run it up to thirty-two pounds. The railroad didn't like that because the maximum weight per crate was supposed to be twenty-eight, but a lot of the shippers loaded the crates and put them in the cars and rolled them. The railroads would send out a young man to weigh the crates and usually they would be around thirty or so, but he wouldn't make a fuss if he'd been on the job a season or two.

It was just no use trying to enforce a rule with grape

shippers. They always got their way, within reason, and when you got down to it, they had a right to. They gave the railroads their best business and it was a tough racket. Usually the shipper lost money, one season or the next, so it was wise to be casual about the crates being heavier than they were supposed to be.

Everybody who was supposed to enforce some kind of a rule discovered sooner or later that it was wisest to take it easy and not try to be an enforcer of law or obnoxious. An old-time railroad man, a vice president or a general manager, would tell a young man just out of college and going to work for the first year, "I know you know the rules, Jim, but let me tell you about Melikian out there at Magunden— well, he knows the rules, too, but you can't keep them, that's all. Sometimes it's just impossible to keep the rules, except you go to work and lose yourself ten thousand dollars, and we figure it's better to break the lousy rule than make a good shipper lose all that money—so take it easy."

I loafed around the packing shed at Magunden where Melikian was loading. Magunden's just outside of Bakersfield and isn't anything but a couple of loading sheds, and a store which is also a lunch room. Of course there is a marble game in the store and a phonograph that plays one of twenty records for a nickel each.

There were three dozen girls and women packing grapes for Melikian, three truckers hauling grapes from the field, a dozen men and boys working with hand trucks, and a half-dozen lidders and loaders. The lidders worked the machine that nailed the lid on the crate; the loaders nailed the crates in the boxcar, over a thousand crates in each car. The grapes were Thompson Seedless, Red Malagas, and Ribiers. Ribiers are those large black grapes that are so good to look at. A well-packed crate of them is something you feel ought to sell for five or six dollars in New York. It is a grape of great beauty, excellent color, and fine flavor, and it is one of the first to ripen. The Thompson is that grape you see at fruit and vegetable markets all the time, either greenish or light brown, and at its best very sweet. In fact you can't eat a lot of this grape because of its sweetness. The Red Malaga is not deep red or anything like that, just something close to red, actually closer to a shade of purple. Ribiers are black with a bloom of dust that makes you admire nature, if you care about such things at all.

All this is in terrific heat which can be delightful if you make no mistakes in eating and drinking. Hard liquor is stupid, and even beer is no good. Soda pop is all right, but best of all is water if you can get good water. The tap water is flat, though, so you have to drink soda pop until you get to a place where there is spring water, out of a jar. Best of all is plain bread and grapes which have been cooled, and once a day a little cold meat. Otherwise in two days you'll feel dopey and the excellent weather will seem fierce—just in case you intend to visit Magunden in August some day and see how the grapes get to market. You probably won't be bothering because in all probability you weren't brought up in the valley and you don't care how they get to market.

The most interesting thing about the grapes getting to market, however, is something I haven't even got close to so far. The innocence. That is, the sort of pardonable unim-

112

aginativeness of the people involved, the Mexicans in the vineyards, the truckers on the road, the shippers in the sheds, the packers, the loaders, the railroad men, the inspectors, and all the others, even the farmers. All these people go to work and get the grapes to New York and other far-away cities without any appreciation for the elemental significance of the ritual. This is so of course because each is troubled by the matter of money. The farmer is worried about what he's going to get, the shipper is always gambling on the market, and the workers of course are working in that heat because they need money to live on. Before the season is half started, though, even the workers have forgotten about living, and are giving everything they've got to the ritual of getting the grapes packed, loaded into the cars, and onto the chain of freight cars that travels across the continent to market. *That* becomes their living. You have only to watch them working around eleven o'clock at night, after twelve or thirteen hours of work, to realize that some of the significance of what's going on has touched them and given them fresh energy to get the last car loaded. They are all simple people, but after many hours of it, the time of year, the temperature, the clearness of the air, and all the other things make them begin to feel that what is happening is not completely an event of business. They work furiously, and nobody stands over them with a whip, nobody tells them what to do or how to do it: they just do it. Melikian told me it could be the slowest-thinking, slowest-moving man in the world, and after three days of it, he would be part of the whole ritual, swift-acting, accurate, and pretty much delighted, if nearly exhausted.

Dear Baby

Only two or three of the three dozen girls and women will seem attractive at first; all the others will seem worn-out, dried-out, ugly and everything else unpleasing, but after you get to know them just a little, you know how truly beautiful each of them is, even the ones who are, at first glance, ugly. The ones which seemed attractive at first will seem almost incredibly intelligent and beautiful after two or three days, which of course is an illusion—the summertime sharpness coming out of all things and bringing them to the top of their form, ripening the grape on the vine in six hours, and intensifying any good thing in anybody almost to the point of perfection.

I'm thinking about the vines in the heat, the bunches of grapes ripening on them, the color and flavor of them, and how they get to the millions of people in the big cities in the East, before summertime ends—giving each of them who wishes to know the taste of the grape a chance to hold a bunch of them by the stem and pluck the berries off and eat them, before it is winter again, before the season is over and there are no grapes anywhere and the vines are all bare. The toughest thing in the world is to feel the summertime depth of ripeness, and then to separate the obvious part of it from the part of it that's truly the truth.

That is the tough part of it, for anybody: the young government inspector who is supposed to see that, when the clerk buys a bunch of grapes in New York, he won't taste sour grapes; the railroad inspector who is supposed to keep the shipper from gypping the railroad out of tariff by loading the boxes too heavily and making the railroad haul a ton extra, free; the girls and women packing the grapes for three cents a crate in order to have a hundred dollars or so at the end of the season; the Mexicans in the field; the truckers; and everybody. To get to the image of the bunch of Ribiers three thousand miles from where they were grown and what they mean to the eye of the Italian bootblack who has brought them home, or anybody.

All this is in the midst of all the other things, each of them of some importance, and yet all of them overlooked, everybody too busy to bother, or too tired, or too poor, or too rich, or too old, or too young, or something else. If it isn't grapes, it's one of the other things, each of them needing to be known about, so that people will know what counts and what doesn't.

But it's too tough a job. What I *wanted* to get was the grapes, the way they are, the way it is, and what I got is something I can't figure out. That was so, most likely, because of the people involved, and what they've been wanting to get, the ones in the heat of the valley, and the ones in the big cities in the East.

They are good people, though, and you know it when you stand in the sharp heat of summertime there and look at the grapes hanging from the vines.

THE FARAWAY NIGHT

This was a day of fog and remembrance of old days and old songs. I sat in the house all afternoon listening to the songs. It was darker everywhere than light and I remembered a song I sang to a girl on a bus once. For a while there we were in love, but when the bus reached Topeka she got off and I never saw her again. In the middle of the night when I kissed her she began to cry and I got sick with the sickness of love. That was a young night in August, and I was on my way to New York for the first time in my life. I got sick because I was going my way and she was going hers.

All this day of fog I sat in the house remembering the way a man's life goes one way and all the other lives another, each of them going its own way, and a certain number of young people dying all the time. A certain number of them going along and dying. If you don't see them again they are dead even if it *is* a small world: even if you go back and look for each of them and find them you find them dead because any way any of them go is a way that kills.

The bus came to Topeka and she got off and walked around a corner and I never saw her again. I saw many others, many of them as lovely as she, but never another like her, never another with that sadness and loveliness of voice, and never another who wept as she wept. There never will be another with her sadness. There never will be an American night like that again. She herself may be lovelier now than then but there will never be another sadness of night like that and never again will she or anyone else weep that way and no man who kisses her will grow sick with the sickness of the love of that night. All of it belongs to a night in America which is lost and can never be found. All of it belongs to the centuries of small accidents, all trivial, all insignificant, which brought her to the seat beside me, and all the small accidents which placed me there, waiting for her.

She came and sat beside me, and I knew the waiting of all the years had been for *her*, but when she got off the bus in Topeka I stayed on and three days later I reached New York.

That's all that happened except that something of myself is still there in that warm, faraway, American night.

When the darkness of day became the darkness of night I put on my hat and left the house. I walked through the fog to the city, my heart following me like a big patient dog, and in the city I found some of the dead who are my friends, and in laughter more deathly and grievous than the bitterest weeping we ate and drank and talked and sang and all that I remembered was the loveliness of her weeping because the years of small accidents had brought us together, and the foolishness of my heart telling me to stay with her and go nowhere, telling me there was nowhere to go.